MEI

KNIGHT

To Laurie,

All the best!

MELODY
KNIGHT
A VAMPIRE'S TALE

A NOVEL BY
TONY LINDSAY

atmosphere press

CHAPTER
- ONE -

After I died, I earned a Bachelor of Science degree from the Illinois Institute of Technology and a Master of Science degree from the University of Chicago. Also, I earned my Oh Dan blackbelt in Taekwondo, and I became a CIA operative. I walked to Jackson, Mississippi, then back home to Chicago out of boredom. Because the lead scientist said a woman couldn't, I spent six weeks in a life pod under the Atlantic to help develop an aqualung that pulled breathable oxygen from ocean water, and I designed a logistics program that sold to FedEx for ten million dollars. Again, I did all this after I died. I knew vampires who called how we existed a curse, and I understood their perspective, but I didn't share it because death gave me life.

- Monday night -

His name was Fernando Castillo, and I hated his guts. He didn't look like a child-murdering monster dressed in his light blue linen suit, and his soft almost seductive smile had no evil residue dripping from it the night he opened the hotel suite door. He looked like a friendly middle-aged Spanish guy.

"It's good to see you again, Ms. Knight" was how he greeted me when I stepped into the suite. Castillo's hand instantly went to the small of my back as we walked to the suite's bar. My sundress, which was twelve inches above my knees, was a bright yellow; a beautiful sunflower yellow that I knew wouldn't remain after cleaning; all I was expecting to get out the dress, in its original radiance, was two wearings at the most. I really didn't want his palm print on the dress, so I stepped out of his reach and walked toward the bar.

He continued past me to the bar. He went behind the bar and started pulling glasses from the single shelf. I sat on one of the two tall barstools.

"Do you, like most African American women, drink rum and Coke?"

I detest being corralled into a group and categorized, and when it happened verbal venom automatically spewed from my mouth, but I was on assignment with a goal in mind, so I tried to curtail the venom.

"I don't think I am like most of any group, and I find it hard to believe that most Black women like rum and Coke. Most of my friends don't even drink." I smiled.

Yes, he needed to die, but information was needed first.

I was trying hard not to think about the suffocated children. Letting my anger show was not an option because I wanted the name of the company that owned the train car; the company that the CIA was protecting. Chad, my handler for the agency, was very detailed in the assignment parameters – information only.

I consulted with my father, Daniel, also a CIA operative, about Castillo's involvement in the death of the children, and his advice was to follow the CIA directives, but I wanted to do more, and those murdered children deserved more.

"Oh, you are one of a kind, a unique beauty, no? I love you proud African American women, independent thinkers, no? Well, there is no Coke available. Is Pepsi and rum ok?"

He was still assuming I drank, and he was still assuming I drank rum and cola. I couldn't immediately kill him because my plan was to go to the press with the name of the company, and after exposing the company, the whole mess would be left to humans to handle. So I said, "That will be fine, thank you," and kept the smile on my face.

"I know that you Americans are very brand conscious, but to me, cola is cola."

"Yes, I agree. Soda is soda, and rum is rum."

He shook his head to the negative, causing his brown hair to wave at me. "Oh no, there is a big difference in rums, but you only have one choice, so your being impartial is a very good thing."

He grabbed the ice for my drink out of the ice bucket without washing his hands, and the sink was right there. After he fixed my drink with his bare unwashed hands, he poured himself a straight shot of tequila.

"It has been a long day," he exhaled, putting the stopper back in the tequila.

He pushed my drink across the narrow bar to my fingers, and he gently slid his index finger across the back of my hand. I had to fight against the reflex of snatching my hand away. Castillo's touch turned my stomach, but my smile held. He came from behind the bar and sat on the barstool next mine.

I purposely hadn't fed, so I smelled the greed in his blood when he sat next to me. The rush of his blood moving through his veins was almost distracting. He uncorked the bottle, poured and downed another shot, and he nosily tapped the shot glass down on the bar top.

"Argh, ok. Now let's talk." He spun all the way around on the barstool like a kid. He stopped and said, "Forgive me, Melody; but why are we meeting this evening? My mind is filled with so many meeting agendas." The same index finger he used to caress the back of my hand circled his temple in a loco motion, "My memory is gone bye-bye." His eyes smiled with his narrow lips.

I put the glass to my own lips but didn't actually sip it. I placed it on the bar and answered him.

"It's concerning the Sierra Lone rejection and cargo contamination."

I looked at his reflection in the bar's mirror. His jet-black hair contrasted against his buttermilk skin. My skin, which shone like chocolate satin, was not reflected in the mirror. In the thirty-seven years that I have existed as a vampire, only one person noticed that I have no reflection in the mirror, a child who is now grown.

When I mentioned Sierra Lone, Castillo lowered his head for a moment.

"Oh yes, a very sad occurrence, so many deceased children."

He seemed sincere in his concern, but I knew better; humans are all deceitful, especially the greedy.

"The problem, sir, is in identifying the owner of the cargo car. If we can do that, your company will avoid any bad press and legal responsibility."

He spent his shot glass on the bar top with his fingertips.

"Yes, I understand, but my PR people and legal team have assured me that Legacy Airlines cannot be held responsible by any means. We merely transported the car. The search for the owners is not our concern, and the government of Sierra Lone understands this, so don't worry your pretty little head about such matters. I have others working on it." He looked up from the spinning shot glass to me. "So, you are from Chicago, no?"

He'd turned on the stool to face me squarely. I was still facing the mirror, and I watched him in the mirror; he was looking at me from head to toe. His gazed lingered on my small breasts.

"I live here; I was born and raised in Atlanta. But, sir, you have been ill advised; international law holds the transporting company responsible for any contamination. As a logistics professional my concern is warranted; we must identify the shipper."

I looked from his reflection in the mirror to his face. The blood of the greedy not only has its own distinct scent, it smells a lot like blue cheese, but it is heavier than non-greedy blood; it weighs more in my stomach. I noticed the difference after my first banker. I confirmed the difference with a billionaire stockbroker. I leave the greedy in death, no living-death for them.

"It's not a problem, Ms. Knight, trust me, as you Americans say."

He was smiling, and then I saw the evil dripping from his Cheshire Cat grin. And my mind moved to the pictures of the suffocated children stacked in that boxcar. I was certain his blood would be very heavy.

"Tell me more about you, Melody. Enough talk of business. I had an African American wife once; she wasn't as beautiful as you, but she was a beauty, but alas she wasn't happy living in Cuba, and I couldn't stomach New York. A skinny, selfish, spoiled woman who was not willing to sacrifice her modeling career to be my wife. The marriage was annulled, and we parted amiably. She did break my heart, into many pieces, but the sex, oh the sex was spectacular."

I exhaled and smiled and sat straighter on the barstool, and then asked, "We are not going to talk about the Sierra Leone, are we?"

He reached again to my hand and caressed the back of it with his fingertips, "No, we are not. I took this meeting because I am looking to hire a personal assistant. My business is requiring me to be in Chicago more than anticipated, and if you are willing?"

The look on his face was not business. Lecherous was the word. His eyes were on my thighs, then again on my breasts, and then back to my thighs. I have the same twenty-two-year-old body and face I had when I was turned.

"What does the position entail?" I forced myself to ask. Perhaps if I got him talking, he might name the owner of the cargo car; that company was just as guilty as he, and I wanted them both destroyed.

"I am very partial to dark women. My current wife is Ethiopian; perhaps it is your skin color that attracts me. I find you very attractive, Melody."

He was still caressing my hand with his fingers.

"I'm flattered, sir. By your attraction and the job offer, but I have a consulting business that takes up much of my time."

"Are we negotiating?" He grinned. His gums were almost black coffee brown. It only took me two weeks to find the evidence of Castillo's human trafficking, but that wasn't what Chad or the CIA wanted.

"No, sir. I am not for hire full-time."

"What about for the evening?"

"Sir?"

"What if I paid you ten thousand dollars to spend the night with me?"

I pulled my hand from his.

"I am not a prostitute, sir."

I'd have rather chewed glass than have had him inside me.

"Twenty thousand dollars?"

His mind was on sex, only. He was not going to talk about the shipment of children or the cargo car owner. I stood from the barstool and pulled the bright yellow dress over my head. I watched his mouth drop open. Thirty some odd years ago, I was concerned about a man's initial opinion of my small breasts even if I was about to feed on the man, but that insecurity is gone. I like my half a lemon-sized breasts, and I love the way they hold a man's attention.

"You can keep your money, sir."

I stepped to his barstool and began kissing his lips and progressed down his chin to his neck.

He was surprised by my sudden approach.

"Twenty thousand, then?" he asked.

I smelled the greed in his blood. After fifty-nine years of

being on this earth, I have seen too much evil done for profit. I abhor the greedy; those that sacrifice the lives of weaker individuals for their own bottom-line disgust me, and children had died for Castillo's profit.

"Lean your head back, sir. And I am not a prostitute, so keep your money."

I returned to giving his neck small kisses.

"Call me Pappi," he said, leaning his head further back. "And I insist that you take the money. No confusion when services are paid for."

I was insulted. But instead of commenting, I placed my lips and tongue so seductively on his neck that he didn't wince when I broke his skin; he only moaned. I didn't want to prolong touching him, but I dropped my hand to his lap to distract him further as my canines dropped wholly into his jugular. He wiggled but continued to moan in satisfaction with my hand in his lap. He lost enough blood to drift into semiconsciousness. His only protest was mumbled words. I fed until there was no more.

When I rose from his neck, he was only skin, bone, and dry muscle; there was not a drop of blood in his corpse. In the bar mirror, his buttermilk skin looked ashen white. He wasn't coming back, no living-death for him. I never gave the greedy the living-death, only the distraught, those that wanted to die. I knew my father would be disappointed. The murderer's death was not what the CIA wanted.

With my stomach bulging with his heavy blood, I searched the suite for his laptop. I found it in a briefcase on his bed. I easily hacked into his files and searched through them until dawn. Chad was certain Castillo was linked to the Cuban Banco Republica that was hindering the CIA plans in the country; the trafficking of human children was not a priority for the agency.

I found more than enough evidence to show his affiliation and part ownership of Cuban Banco Republica. Chad and his superiors would be pleased. I also discovered that the American company that owned the shipping car was partly owned by Legacy Airlines, Castillo's airline. That information I forwarded to Thomas Adomako, the child that noticed I casted no reflection in a mirror. He had become a reporter at the *Chicago Tribune.*

I walked to the balcony and pushed the hotel's glass doors open. Castillo's suite was on the twenty-first floor, and the view was breathtaking. The cool dawn air was titillating. My nipples became erect. I had time to dress and leave the hotel by normal means before daybreak, but the brisk dawn air really appealed to me, and Castillo's scent was heavy on my yellow dress. I wanted no parts of him near me again, so I left the dress. The thought of free-falling nude from the balcony was irresistible. I took flight in the dawn.

Sixteen children died due to his greed. He was a trusted dignitary, a rising political star, but no more. I snuffed his celestial flicker with no remorse. My contracted CIA assignment was to observe and report, but Chad only involved me in kill missions; so despite his politically tempered words and careful instructions to "Please, observe and report only," I wasn't expecting any blowback from the kill, and the shearing brisk air from the twenty-first-story drop stripped away any doubts concerning the righteousness of Castillo's death. He deserved to die.

I wasn't the only vampire racing against the sun between Chicago skyscrapers. I swooshed in a downdraft at jet speed and didn't slow down at street level. I blazed down the sidewalk like a meteor.

I went through the cat's flap like a missile, and I spun down the dryer vent tube onto the bare mattress; all of these entry items were installed and prepared for me by Calvin Melrose: the cat-flap, the dryer tube, and the mattress. On the mattress, I forced myself to calm down before transforming from cloud to woman. The first year after I was given the gift transformation was painful, but not any longer; it was like taking a morning stretch.

After I wholly transformed, I rolled naked from the mattress to the concrete cellar floor and lay face down. The cold concrete pleased me; above the cellar was a deli, owned by one of my minions, Calvin Melrose. I turned my head to the left, lying on my right cheek. My father communicated with each of his daughters, my two sisters, telepathically. When I wanted to reach him, all I had to do was think of speaking to him.

"Father?" my request left my mind.

"Yes, Melody." He answered immediately.

"I fed on the man responsible for the dead children."

"Yes … I thought you might. Children have your heart."

"I am questioning my involvement with the CIA; their interests are different from mine."

"I understand, but I ask that you wait two months before making a decision; plans are being orchestrated that may change your thoughts about the agency, and I need you where you are with Chad. Just be patient, daughter. A change is coming."

My father had been with the CIA since its inception; his loyalties were not mine. My thoughts were concerned with immediate action; I wanted out and away from the CIA as soon as possible, but what I said was, "Ok, father, I will stay for two months."

"Thank you, Melody," and our telepathic conversation ended.

Castillo owned the cargo airline, but an American company owned the cargo train car where the children were found, and the CIA refused to investigate further. Yesterday, I went to Chad's office and filed the report about the dead children, and the report ended with him. He called the report "ancillary knowledge" and not the focus of my assignment. I was to find information linking Castillo to the Cuban Banco Republica, nothing more. All I said in response to his callousness was "fucking humans" and left his office.

I rolled over on my back; the night had been productive, and I easily drifted into a peaceful rest.

CHAPTER
- TWO -

My human life ended on my wedding day, two days after my twenty-second birthday. But before my death, my human life had taken me low.

As a student of history, I was saddened by and greatly disappointed in the actions of humanity. The repeated atrocities of mankind depressed me. My belief in a benevolent omnipotent God and my faith in man's ability to follow the Golden Rule lessened with my education. The more I learned, the more I studied ... the more I doubted the human race's ability to do good, and the less I believed in a superior being that had man's best interest as a concern. I became depressed with the knowledge that man, that humanity, was on its own.

Genocides, planet destruction, racism, land dominance,

slavery, and continuous wars all weighed heavily on my thoughts and beliefs. I was considering dropping out of school because knowledge was not feeling like power; it felt like accountability, and I was powerless to balance the ledgers. I was human, but I couldn't right the wrongs of humanity, and it appeared historically obvious that there was no superior being to correct the wrongs.

My study of history told me that too much wrong had been done, and it appeared that people would continue to hurt each other, and they would continue to destroy the planet. I was beaten down by historical events, but then I met Christopher.

He was high school dropout, and he had no training as a therapist, but one day he walked into my family's shoe shop, and he took one look at me and said, "Let it go – whatever you are holding onto is dragging you through a bunch of shit." I stood there at that counter and cried because my studying was dragging through shit, through the waste of humanity.

I didn't want Christopher to see me crying because I knew who he was. He was the only person in our neighborhood that drove a big new Mercedes Benz. He was a drug dealer, but he saw my tears, and he saw my sadness.

The next time I saw him he brought me purple and yellow roses. I threw them in the trash with him standing at the counter. When he left, I took them out, and he immediately came back into store and saw me with the roses. He had forgotten to leave the shoes for polishing. We went out that night.

I saw his drug dealing, which I hated, and I saw his obsessive desire for wealth. We dated for four months, clearly seeing each other, and we fell in love despite the *seeing.*

Being in love with Christopher brightened my perspective, and I became hopeful that the world could change. But then … man killed my love and my despair returned.

We had a beautiful wedding day: there was sun, robins, cherry blossoms, limos, and photographers. Christopher arrived in a black limo with his groomsmen, and I arrived in a white one with my bridesmaids. As planned, my bridesmaids and I exited our limo first and walked into the field house. We hadn't made it to the front desk when rapid gunshots rang out. Men in ski masks with machine guns were standing in the sun shooting down everyone in front of the field house.

There was no glass left in the black limo. Only the gunmen were standing. Groomsmen and my groom lay dead and bloody on the cobblestone sidewalk and in the spring green grass. The shooters even killed the squirrels. They turned their guns to us standing behind the field house glass doors; others ran, I stood still, but they didn't fire. They lowered their weapons and loaded into two black SUVs and drove off.

- Tuesday night -

"Sister Melody, Sister Melody, outside, outside! There are two slayers! Do you hear me, Sister?"

Calvin was pleading more than questioning, and yes, I heard him. I heard him pacing the deli after he said goodnight to his workers walking back and forth from the front windows to the trap door. My eyes opened at sundown, but my ears hadn't closed: I heard his first customer sipping coffee, I heard his two workers punching in and punching out, I heard him dicing celery, I heard a customer in the bathroom shaving her eyebrow pencil, and I heard a very sick man injecting himself. I heard everything. Calvin had turned both the front door's keyless tumbler locks and walked behind the counter. He was standing still behind the counter probably looking out at the slayers.

"Sister Melody?" He asked again. He knew I heard him, but the slayers had him unsettled.

Even though they were across the street, the scent of the slayers filled my head; they smelled like earth, like soil. They lived and worked on farms, but they were not farmers, they were slayers, destroyers of vampires.

Calvin pulled the rubber mat back and opened the trap door. He began descending heavily down the stairs to the hidden basement room. He became my minion because of his family. I was drawn to him to feed because his despair reeked through the air. He wanted to die, and he had a .45 in his pocket to help him with the task. But after tracking him to his home, I watched his children greet him with glee despite the meager trappings in their dilapidated home. Seeing he had four daughters and a wife with no job, no money, and no car, I understood why he reeked of despair. Feeding from him would only have only added to his family's woes.

Calvin was a stout man, a wide man with watermelon thick biceps and skin the color of a lion's hide. He had what my mother called "negro" features: a broad nose, thick lips, and a raised forehead. He didn't look like a man who would put a gun to his own head four nights in a row, but he did.

The first night his oldest daughter needed help with her

homework and that stopped his suicide. The next night a mouse ran through the house and set the females in a state of panic. The third night the baby woke up crying because she peed in the bed. The fourth night his wife needed him to help with the ironing. The fifth night I passed through the slightly cracked porch window, and when I transformed from cloud to naked woman, he dropped the .45 and called me Sister Madonna. I told him my name was Melody, but he has refused to drop the Sister title.

When he stepped from the last step to the concrete floor of the basement, I told him, "Yes, they have been out there for hours. They came into the store twice. They know I am here, and that's to their misfortune; tonight, two white-eyed slayers will die."

I rose from the concrete floor, and Calvin walked to the metal wardrobe and pulled out clothes for me. Calvin had fought slayers with me in the past.

"Why did they stay? It's sundown. Why didn't they approach during the day?" He handed me a black running suit and a pair of Roman sandals.

"Uncertain of numbers" was my reply. "They didn't know who would fight with me. Now, they count only you and I, and they have probably called for reinforcements, but those two out there will die."

While I dressed, he went to the locked wall cabinet with stainless steel doors. He entered his code and the door opened. He retrieved my Viking and Falchion swords. He pulled out a Roman Gladius and Colt .45 for himself. He dropped two loaded clips into the pocket of his jeans and inserted one into the Colt.

"You should take this .9mm." He tried to hand me a black Beretta.

"Not tonight." I zipped up the jacket and tightened the straps on the sandals. I stood straight up and picked up the swords from the table. "I think I will be finished before you make it across the street." With swords in hand, I was up the stairs and out the door before he could take a step.

The slayers had drawn their bows, and when they sensed me, they released arrows toward the door. I passed through both sets like wind. They were obviously hoping for additional help before I got to them. Fear made them both fumble with drawing more arrows. They dropped their bows and drew swords, and they were both skilled fighters just human and too slow. One was skilled enough to block two of my strikes. The other I beheaded with the first slash; he died more from fear than my blade. The older one had fought vampires before; he didn't try to compete in speed. He fought offensive and predictive; he knew how to protect his life but not how to injure me. I was amused by his skill. A silenced shot fired, and the bullet zipped by my ear. The blind slayer's head snapped back, and he dropped to his knees then fell on his face to the sidewalk. Calvin took the slayer's life from across the street with the .45. He was indeed a good minion.

I zipped back across the street and left the bloodied swords at Calvin's feet. Increasing my speed, I transformed and took flight, freeing myself from the running suit and Roman sandals. Less than forty-five seconds had passed during the battle. And to the four sets of horrified slow human eyes that passed by on the street, it looked like the two slayers had attacked each other. Maybe the police would get to the corpses before the other slayers, but whichever way it worked out, the dead bodies didn't concern me. The carcasses were a human problem.

* * *

Because my condominium is the thirty-third-floor penthouse, I was able to run a fresh air duct vent from the roof of the building into my office. Through the air duct is how I enter my home most nights to the paramount confusion of the doormen and security officers; for five years, as long as I have lived in this condominium, both the doormen and the guards have begged me to tell them how I entered undetected by their trusted cameras or motion sensors. I told them I was a witch, and after the second year most of them began to believe me.

The new head of security went as far as installing two additional cameras on my floor by the exit doors. She told me she didn't believe in witches, and it would be only a matter of time before she found the glitch in the system; two years passed and she was still looking.

The fresh air duct took a forty-five-degree angle down from my ceiling; the slide down into my home onto the carpet of my office was rather gentle. Once in, I transformed from my gaseous state to human and stretched towards the ceiling. Not being impeded by the darkness, I seldom notice if a room is lit or dark until light is added or removed. As I stretched, finishing the transformation, I noticed that light was added to my office.

"So, you killed him." The words were dry and very matter of fact.

Chad Oliver had turned on my desk lamp. He was sitting in my chair at my desk as if he was in his own office. I had warned him before about entering my home uninvited.

"And I know it was you who leaked the freight company's name with Castillo's to the press. The story has gone viral; it is trending in all the news sources. Legacy Airlines and Rolland Freight are trading in the toilet, and both corporations have been linked to dying children. That wasn't what the agency wanted."

He wasn't yelling, but his voice was tight with tension. He was leaning back in my leather office chair.

"If you keep entering my home unannounced, one day you are going to see something that will disturb your human mind."

I didn't like Chad, but I didn't hate him. I detested his job, and at times it was difficult for me to separate the man from the position. If it weren't for Daniel's insistence that we help humans, I would have walk away from CIA work after the first assignment.

"Yeah, you mean like bones, tendons, veins, and green gel like blood spreading from a ball of fire and forming a woman. Disturbing like that?"

I turned my head to face him and allowed my eyes to illuminate red; the sight leaves humans unsettled. He adjusted himself in my chair, and I saw him considering his situation. Pseudo supremacy disregarded; Chad knew where the power lay between us.

"Why are you here, Chad?"

He took his hand from my antique iron and brass banker's lamp and exhaled.

"There is nothing that surprises me about you vampires, not even your obstinate refusal to follow agency directives. Your orders were to observe and report, nothing more. We needed Castillo alive and his company prospering."

I lowered my arms from stretching and considered leaving the office and Chad. In my judgment, Castillo didn't deserve to live, so I killed him, and I provided the agency the information they requested. I didn't feel like being reprimanded by someone I helped.

"Those children needed their lives, and he allowed them to suffocate."

Neither Chad nor the CIA cared about dead children, but I did.

"Yeah, well shit happens. One of your ilk was feeding off of infants and delivering mothers at the county hospital. Every living thing on this planet is fucked up, so please stop with the overkill concern about those damn kids in that freight car. Jesus, twenty kids just died in a Syrian bombing this morning. Are you going to flap your little bat wings over to the Pentagon and suck down some blood from one of the joint chiefs of staff? Fucking kids die every day in this fucked up world, but we have to follow orders."

He wasn't quite yelling, but he was loud and returned to leaning back in my chair.

"And put on some clothes." He snapped out the words, turning his blue eyes away from me.

I crossed my arms across my chest and stood still. I considered slapping him hard enough to break his jaw. Leaning forward, I exhaled, "You are an uninvited guest in my home; if my being naked makes you uncomfortable, leave. You arrogant shit."

I walked over to my oak daybed and sat. I thought of gapping my thighs, but I crossed my legs at the knees.

Chad was intrusive. For a human, he was tolerable on most days, but when he let CIA directives rule over his thinking, when he allowed the job to dictate his behavior, I couldn't bear being in his company.

"The last time I checked, the agency was paying the mortgage on this penthouse, so I am never uninvited."

He rocked forward in the chair and attempted a superior managerial attitude which may have worked if we both didn't know that I had enough wealth to buy the building and the whole city block that it sat upon.

"Why are you here, Chad?" I stopped myself from adding – you stupid, little, blond, bureaucratic peon.

He rocked the chair up to the desk and lowered his head and his shoulders slumped. "There is talk. Talk concerning slayers. Pike – and the appropriations committee – feels that there needs to be a stronger check and balance system between humans and vampires.

The issue is control. They can control human agents; that is not the case with vampire agents as Castillo's death indicted to them. Agency goals are not priorities for vampire agents, and that behavior needs to be checked."

It was unexpected and unintentional, but I started laughing. "Are you kidding me?"

I saw his teeth clench and the jaw muscles in his cheeks tightening. "No, I'm not. The talk is that slayers may add to the check and balance needed in the relationship with your kind."

I was so tired of the CIA.

"You mean with us helping you, because that is the relationship. We do what we do to help you – no vampire needs the agency."

He placed his hands palm down on my desk. "I understand the relationship, but Pike and the others are seeking leverage."

Pike was his boss, and I believed Pike worked with my father, but Chad was saying the name as if it would garner respect from me, and it didn't.

"How can there be leverage when we are helping you?"

He sat quiet, and I was looking hard at him, hoping my stare would cause him to rise and leave; it didn't. Instead, he revealed the reason he was in my home.

"We need to arrange a meeting with Daniel and the committee."

Again, he needed something from me, the vampire. "Then do it."

Chad scratched the slight stubble on his cheek and chin. "He won't return our calls, text, or emails."

That meant Daniel didn't want to be bothered and Chad knew that. "He probably knows what you want, and he is obviously not in agreement."

He scooted the chair all the way up to the desk and sat a little more upright in the chair. "You see, that is the problem, Melody. He doesn't have to agree. He just has to follow orders like any other agent."

Again, I laughed. "Oh, I see. And you are right. That is the problem; the fact that you think he is 'like any other agent' is the problem. You and your agency are devaluing a powerful asset, and I won't have any part in it. I only help you because of my father's insistence."

Chad joined both his small effeminate hands together into one fist and bobbed it up and down on my desk. A nervous tic I'd seen him do hundreds of times before.

"Please, just arrange a meeting. The committee is offering an option of two dates; this Friday or next Monday at any time on either date."

I stood from the daybed and walked over to him at my desk. Looking down at him, I asked, "Does the agency really believe the slayers could balance the relationship?"

He shook his blond head no and yes, but he didn't look up at me. "I don't know, but I do know that all parties need to talk if any type of cooperation is to continue."

I was tired of finding Chad in my home. I was tired of providing information that serviced rich corporations and wealthy owners. I was tired of working with an agency that I knew promoted wars and unrest across the globe for capitalistic gain, and I was tired of Chad sitting at my desk.

"Ok, I will reach out to Daniel and get back to you."

Through my telepathic relationship with Daniel, my thinking about him was me reaching out to him.

I told Chad, "I need my desk."

Chad stood, and I saw he was disheveled: his white oxford shirt was only half tucked in, his tie was loosely knotted and looped the front of his shirt, and his fly was half open, but his navy-blue suit was made of beautiful wool.

CHAPTER
- THREE -

Before I met Daniel, my vampire father, I was indeed hopeless. My fiancée, Christopher, had been shot dead. Three hours later, I stood in my bedroom dressed in my justifiably white wedding gown. I shook out eleven blue and white sleeping pills from the bottle in my hand. They were in the center of my palm. Eternal sleep was the answer.

On the dresser was a bottle of spring water. Christopher insisted on spring water. I put the pill bottle on the dresser with my right hand and grabbed the water bottle with my left. When the cloud entered, I thought it was smoke, but it settled on top of the dresser, and I saw flame in its center. It floated to the floor, but I didn't care.

I gathered the pills with my palm and opened my mouth, but the cloud started growing and it touched my feet. I stepped away and watched the transformation. A naked man stood before me, and I could not have cared less. I tilted my head back and opened my mouth, but the pills were gone; they were no longer in my palm. I looked to the floor, but they weren't there. I hadn't dropped them.

The man spoke, "It's not an ending you need but a beginning." He was at my neck in a blink, and I didn't care. I felt his bite and his sucking. I dropped to my knees and he went down with me and continued to feed from my neck. I fell into a sleep.

* * *

I woke naked in the back of limo.

The gas cloud man was sitting beside me. He said, "Don't be afraid." I passed out again.

I clearly heard my heart beating, but I didn't open my eyes; the thumping was reassuring, and it lulled me until it stopped. When I could no longer hear my heart, I opened my eyes, and it started again, but the beat, the thumping, was different, it was faster. I sat up in a bed, a big bed. The cloud man was sitting in chair at a small table with one candle. My vision wasn't blurry as it always was when I woke. Everything I saw seemed pristine despite the room being lit by a single candle.

"Every part of you will be better. You have nothing to fear from the darkness."

I sat all the way up. The sheets were black satin.

"You are in my home. This is my room. You will have your own room if you decide to stay."

I stood with almost no effort. I felt light – as if I weighed nothing and floating was possible. I rose up on my toes and sprung up from the tips. I rose high enough to touch the ceiling ever so lightly. I drifted, drifted, back to the floor like a feather. I stood looking at him, and I remembered.

"You bit me."

"I did."

"I know what you are."

"What we are."

I looked down at my nakedness.

"Where is my gown?"

"With your old life, behind you in Atlanta."

He stood up. He was tall and dark, so dark that I could barely see his skin, but his teeth and eyes were bright. He walked over to the bed.

"We are connected, Melody Knight." I heard him as if he spoke.

"My name is Tasha Lewis." I was talking but no words passed my lips.

"No longer; you are now my Melody."

"You are crazy."

He laughed in my head.

I moved away from him and the bed, and I was surprised by the power in my steps. I ran to the door with the slightest movement. I opened the door, expecting protest from the tall dark man.

The bedroom was dark, but the house beyond the door was well lit. We were on the second floor of the house. I stepped into the hall and closed the door behind me.

"You are not a prisoner, but here with us is the best place for you." He spoke in my head. Hearing him and not seeing him did not shock me. I was without fear. I saw two other doors and the stairs down. I moved toward the stairs.

"Are you going to leave naked?"

I stopped midway down the stairs. I was butt naked.
"Rest."

I was suddenly very tired. I could barely keep my eyes
open. I went down the stairs to an easy chair next to a lamp.
I sat and rested.

- Tuesday night -

I had the ability to just leave and not be bothered with the
CIA. I could have resided in any country I desired, and I was
reminding my father of that fact.

"There are places on earth to live that are outside of the
Central Intelligence Agency's concern: Iceland, Savannah,
Greenland, Ecuador, Trinidad, Antiqua, Singapore, Kiribati
– I don't have to be near them."

"It is not a matter of having to; it is a matter of helping.
We have assisted America for centuries."

I rocked back in my office chair and spun the pen on the
glass shield that covered my oak desktop. It occurred to me
that I didn't know where Daniel was.

"They want to meet with you."

"I know. They want oversight and rule over our actions.
They want to direct us as they do other agents and
contractors."

I had rocked back further in my chair and was unable to
reach the pen.

"And?"

"They are justified in that desire. We are offering them
assistance; they should direct our actions."

"Why haven't you met with them?"

"They want slayers to oversee us, and I view that as a

threat. I won't meet with slayers, but I want you to."

"What?" I sat erect.

"I want you to go on my behalf and listen to what they propose, both of them, the slayers and the agency. Charlette and Juanita will go with you."

"That is not something I want to do."

"I am aware, but you will."

And he was gone from my mind as quickly as he entered. Me meeting with the agency would allow him to be there without being agitated by their demands. I leaned forward in my chair and spun the black Montblanc pen again on my desk. Charlette and Juanita, my sisters, contracted with the agency as well. I was certain neither one of them would be happy about meeting with slayers.

Daniel must be aware of some type of deception to send them with me. My desk phone chirped like a spring robin. I designed the ringtone myself. As Thomas Adomako's name displayed on the data screen, I picked up the phone.

"Greetings. How is my favorite newspaper reporter?"

"Doing well, Melody. How are you?"

"I'm good – what's up?" I knew he was calling about the information I sent him on Castillo and the Cuban Banco Republica.

"As always, I appreciate the information you send my way; however, this last story has ruffled some unexpected feathers. It appears that the corpse of Fernando Castillo was found this afternoon in a hotel suite. The information you sent me was sent from his laptop after his estimated time of death. The city police are pressuring me for information. Two detectives came to see me, a Moss and a Bowman. I told them the source was anonymous, but that detective – the fortyish-year-old one with acne, Detective Moss – was very suspicious, and he linked his questions to past deaths that I reported on. The articles about corpses that were drained dry of bodily fluids.

"He said Castillo didn't even have sperm left in his ball sack, and that there was no moisture in his bones, and that he was nearly dust. I told him that I had no knowledge of Castillo's demise, but he wasn't convinced. He brought your name up before he left. He asked if you were involved in my receiving the information. Of course, I said no, but he knew your name."

I spun the pen again.

"Yes, we have crossed paths twice before. Detective Moss washed out of training as a slayer. He refused the blindness, so he knows my kind exists. He is not a threat, but thank you for the warning."

"Melody?"

"Yes?"

"Do be careful; whether you view this detective as a threat or not, he stated your name with animosity, and he spoke as if already knew you were involved."

I opened my laptop and the file on Detective Ulises Moss.

"No worries, Thomas, and I appreciate your concern. How are Tammy and the twins?"

Detective Ulises Moss's picture appeared on my scene, with a gray and black twist in his hair and a stern expression on his bronzed face. He did hate me, but he wasn't the first, and he wouldn't be the last.

"They are well. Tammy is annoyed by my late hours here; she doesn't always believe work keeps me away. She thinks I am shirking my fair share of time with the twins, and she is right. I do prefer reporting to bottle duty and baby burping and rocking, but please keep that between us."

I couldn't help but laugh; Thomas loved his job, and he was good at it.

"I remember burping you, such a greedy boy you were. I am sure your sons have your appetite."

Thomas's mother, Tina Adomako, was my only female minion.

"Mother often told me how you spent hours with me as a baby, but my first memory of you was not seeing you, not seeing you in that mirror, and in my young mind, I accepted it as normal because Mother told me you were my godmother. So, I figured you were special, and I was right.

"Jesus, I'm tired. All of us are not nocturnal beings. I'm heading home; be careful, Melody. We love you and need you."

I didn't love him or need him, but I understood his human emotion, and his words made me smile.

"Goodnight, Thomas."

I added Detective Moss to my list of reasons for wanting to leave America. He wasn't a threat; he was an annoyance. My desk phone chirped again. It was the doorman's station.

"There is a Calvin Melrose to see you, Ms. Knight." It was the security chief Jocelyn Warren, the one who said she didn't believe in witches and who promised to find out how I entered the building, calling from the doorman's desk.

"Send him up."

It was unusual for her to be working the doorman's desk.

As a minion, Calvin still required human food, and he was mostly human. He didn't feed on human blood to survive. Replacing my vampire blood with the small about of blood I took from him increased his strength and stamina. He didn't have to sleep, but he could if he chose to. He could not transform, but he could run down a speeding car and break any man's back.

I opened the door, and he walked through my condominium door without a greeting and went straight to the office section. The only doors in my condo were on the bathrooms and the front door. In my office space, he paced in front of my desk. I sat behind the desk, waiting.

"Sister Melody, the police came to my home, two detectives, Moss and Bowman. They had video footage of the slayers' deaths. You are a not seen, but they have me firing the pistol and the swords dropping at my feet. I am on video picking up the swords and going back into the café. That Moss guy said he knows I am one of your minions. He said I was going to hell for consorting with a demon.

"They searched the café but didn't find the trapdoor, so they didn't find anything. The other detective, the Magnum P.I. looking one, Bowman, wanted to arrest me due to the video, but there were no bodies or blood. The slayers got there minutes after you left and washed it all down.

"Moss knew that; he knew all about the slayers. He said to tell you that he knows you killed Fernando Castillo and justice for demons is hell."

I started laughing, hard and loud. Calvin collapsed to the daybed sitting prone and not laughing. "What is funny, Sister Melody?" he asked.

The police coming to his home had Calvin unsettled. He loved his family and would sacrifice anything for them. I made him a minion because of his family love. I looked over at Moss's stern face on my laptop scene and closed the file.

"He thinks I am demon. I forget slayers believe that. Their beliefs are just as slow as their movements. You feared the detectives? You, a man who has killed slayers, feared police detectives?"

We looked into each other's eyes. I admired that he didn't look away.

"Moss caught me off guard with his knowledge and the video clip, Sister. But yes, I feared them both. They could have arrested me and destroyed my life."

I nodded my head a little, agreeing with him.

"They could have arrested you, and I would have removed you from their jail. You are larger than them. You are with me; no human or human system has dominion over you."

His admitted fear signaled weakness to me. I swooshed across the room and immediately fed on him until he passed out. When he woke, I fed him half a gauntlet of my blood.

"Never, ever, fear man." I told him as he gulped my blood from the crystal gauntlet.

CHAPTER
- FOUR -

Upon rising the next evening, I couldn't float to the ceiling. I was barely able to stand. My legs cramped terribly, and my fingers and toes were stiff with pain. Standing straight sent pain from the back of my neck to the back of my calves, and there was an odor in the room; it smelled like a small dead animal was close. When I looked to my hands, I noticed my fingernails had grown to look like claws. I heard Daniel in my head as he and two women entered the bedroom. The women would become sisters.

"Time to feed."

The bald woman with huge breasts, Charlette, brought clothes to me: jeans, a yellow sweatshirt, and a black pair of Air Force One's; no panties, socks, or bra – not that I wore bras often, but I would've liked to have had the choice. Daniel laughed inside my head at the thought.

The other woman, Juanita, was as charcoal dark as Daniel, and her straight black hair shone like glass, and it hung down to her elbows. She walked to me and said, "You will watch me feed first. The first one will be entirely mine. The second one I will start for you. The next one you will start and finish on your own. Understand?"

She spoke to me as if I was stupid. I decided not to answer and to look away from her, which was a mistake. She grabbed the hair at the back of my head and snatched me to the floor. Pain shot through my whole body. She slung me around the floor like a mop. When she stopped, I couldn't utter a protest or form an argumentative thought. I was wrecked.

"You will listen to me, for what I tell you and show you will allow you to exist. Death is trying to reclaim you; you reek of it. Learn or rot and perish."

When she released my hair, I was too weak to stand. Daniel picked me up from the floor and carried me out to the limo. I slumped into a corner against a window and looked into the night at unfamiliar streets. I had forgotten we had left Atlanta and were in Chicago.

"Alexander, drive to the Excalibur Gentleman's Club first; there should be low-hanging fruit there." Daniel's voice sounded harsher when spoken. The driver, Alexander, who could have been Shaquille O'Neal's twin, garnered my attention. He smelled good to me; it was like I smelled ribs on the grill or toast being browned in butter; he smelled like food, and I found myself sitting up.

"No, no, Melody. Alexander is my minion and not a meal for you." Daniel was in my head. I slumped back down as we progressed through the unfamiliar city.

"Here, stop here." The coal dark woman, Juanita, addressed Alexander. He pulled the limo to the curb. She looked at me. "I am going to bring one to your window. Look very closely at where I begin feeding."

A minute or so later, Juanita was at my window with a fat white man with black hair. He didn't have on any pants, and he looked to be drunk or in a daze. She put her hand on his forehead and leaned his head back. She slapped his neck and his vein rose; it looked huge to me, and it was obvious were she was going to feed. I smelled the fat man's blood through the window while she feed. She finished him like a juice box, and he just dropped to the ground. He was no longer fat.

Juanita got back into the limo, and Alexander drove off. Her stomach was expanded as if she was six months pregnant.

"Oh, I wasn't expecting a porker. Charlette, you are going to have to start for Melody. I am done." She stretched back and extended her legs and sighed.

Charlette, the bald one with the big breasts, laughed, "You could have shared the piggy with her."

"I could have, but I didn't, so you are up."

Charlette continued laughing, and she directed Alexander to "park in the next alley, and Melody, you come with me."

I heard nothing from Daniel, who was smiling and looking at Juanita.

When the limo stopped in the alley, Charlette got out and I didn't hesitate in following. I was hungry, and I smelled garlic in butter sauce. We walked further into the dark alley, and the lights from the limo faded, but I was able to see clearly; there were three prostitutes on their knees servicing men. It didn't make sense to me; the appealing smell was coming from them.

"What do you smell?" Charlette asked.

"Garlic in melting butter."

"Good, the garlic is sex. The butter is fresh blood. Death changes how we smell. Do you smell the decay?"

I did and it was getting stronger.

"Yes."

"That scent is coming from you; it can only be stopped by feeding. We are fire, and blood feeds the flame. When your flame lessens, decay begins to claim you."

I heard her, and I knew she was trying to give me information, but I was being overcome by hunger. My stomach cramped, and I was dizzy with the need for sustenance, and the people in the alley smelled like lasagna to me, especially the closest couple. I could no longer wait for instruction. The man was lasagna, and I attacked him.

I yanked him from the prostitute and gorged into his neck. I had more flesh in my mouth than blood. I chewed more than drank, but once his juggler was pierced, and his blood flowed into my mouth, I slowed down and drank. The prostitute panicked, but Charlette was on her before she could scream and disrupt the commerce of the alley. I had torn the man's vocal cords from his neck. When he collapsed to the ground, I went down with him. I fed until there was no more.

"What a mess." I heard Daniel in my head. He was standing over me. "We must never let the thirst overcome our intellect. You fed like a dog." He snatched me up from my first feeding and dragged me back to the limo. The other prostitutes and their customers were fleeing the alley as well.

"That is not how it is done," I heard Daniel saying.

- Wednesday -

After Calvin left my home, I pulled my smart phone from the top desk drawer and sent Chad a text:

Friday 7 p.m. your offices.

With Daniel? he asked.

Through me, I replied.

Fine, was his response.

I put the phone back in my drawer and pushed it closed. It wouldn't have been that difficult to leave the US. My business was in my laptop and in my mind. My minions could've chosen to leave with me or return to being human. Father would've been the problem. He could've command me to stay, and I would have been stuck. My fortune was earned in America, but I felt no loyalties to the nation. My attention returned to my laptop, and I opened an email account.

There were four messages from Marcus Lane, my minion pilot and business partner. The first email was confirming my flight in our new chopper; I confirmed. The next email was from a Japanese exporting company that could not get freight into Ghana; that was a simple logistics problem for me. I worked with shipping companies in both Japan and Ghana, and my logistics company, Pirate International, owned four cargo jets. Thomas's mother opened up the African continent for me twenty years ago. Being Ghanaian, she started with Ghana. The Japanese company's problem was easy money for me. It took three phone calls to Japan, three emails, and four calls to Ghana to net $750,000.

When I stood from my desk and stretched, I heard my front door buzz. I looked to my wall clock; it read 2:40 a.m., and the door being buzzed indicated an internal visitor; someone within the building was visiting. When I got to my front door, I smelled earth, soil. The scent was as strong as a slayer.

I opened the security screen console above the light switch and saw the lean, athletic face of Jocelyn Warren, the condominium's director of security. I had smelled earth on her before, but never that strong. I checked the monitor again; it was only Jocelyn in the hall. I opened the door.

Her brown hair was cut short, like a marine. She had on beige khakis and a white Nike mesh T-shirt was spread across her broad shoulders. She was easily six four. In her hand was an iPad.

"Good day, Ms. Knight; could you give me a minute?"

Her words were asking, but her manor was demanding. She took the first step into my place without waiting for me to respond. I had to put my hand on her chest to stop her advance. She stopped.

"I would like to review some videos with you." She held up the iPad.

"Come in," I allowed her to enter and closed the door behind her. She took two steps and stopped. She turned around to face me.

"I grew up in Iowa. I was raised on a farm."

That explained the smell of earth. Farmers kept the scent of soil.

"Four miles from my family's farm was a facility where people were trained to kill vampires; at least that was the town myth. As I teenager, I thought it was all bullshit. When

I went away to college and returned to the farm, I considered the people in the facility a cult. I didn't believe that their beliefs were based in reality. Yesterday, two Chicago police detectives came to see me, and one, a Detective Moss, asked questions about you, and the questions made me think of home.

"Six weeks ago, I installed three video cameras on the roof; one pointing at the fresh air duct you requested for cooking ventilation. You are not a witch, Ms. Knight."

She paused and looked directly into my eyes.

"You are a vampire. It wasn't until I fought with Iraqi soldiers that I accepted the existence of your kind. I have seen balls of fire transform into men. I have fought in combat with vampires at my side."

She handed me the iPad.

"Here are six weeks of videos of a cloud entering your requested air duct. I did not surrender these videos to the Chicago police because vampires saved my life, twice. I don't trust your kind, but I don't consider you an enemy, and I know the Central Intelligence Agency pays your mortgage, so you must not be an enemy of this nation. I just wanted you to know that I am no longer concerned about your comings and goings."

She stepped past me, and her exit was just as bold as her entrance.

"You can leave the iPad at the desk when you finish."

I stopped her.

"Here, take it with you. I have no need to watch myself entering my home."

She smiled at me, but I didn't return it. She took the iPad and said, "I told you I would figure it out." She left with the satisfied smile still on her face.

I heard my phone vibrating in my desk drawer. I closed the front door and quickly walked back to my desk. Juanita's name was on the screen. It took years for us to get close. I hold grudges, and the anger from the initial beating she gave me remained with me for quite a while; it wasn't until we spent six weeks together under the Atlantic Ocean working on the aqualung that my grudge subsided. She was part of the research team that was led by a sexist scientist who believed women could not work long periods of time in confined spaces; it was her idea to prove him wrong, and she invited me to take part.

"Hey," I answered as I sat.

"Hello, I just spoke to Daniel. Did you set the meeting?"

"Yeah, it's set for seven Friday night."

"Did you call Charlette?"

"No."

"Do, because she is in Puerto Rico and will need time to get here. Are we meeting at your place prior?"

She asked, but it was a directive. She has never stopped giving me orders.

"Yes, that will be fine."

"Slayers – what the hell is the CIA thinking?"

"Father thinks control."

"As if slayers can control us; they have been dying at the hands of vampires for centuries."

"And we theirs," was my reply.

"Only the weak and feeble; an astute vampire has never been killed by a slayer. When was the last time you saw Charlette?"

"Two or three years ago, she pulled me into protecting some doctors in Libya. Why?"

"She is discontent, saying two hundred years is too

much life for one person. She is tired of the living-death."

"No, not Charlette. She thrives on this existence."

"No more, and even Daniel couldn't change her attitude. She told him he cursed her, and he should have let her die two hundred years ago."

"Why? What happened to get her thinking that way?"

"Existing two hundred years is my guess."

I leaned back in my office chair.

"But there are others who have existed longer, five, six hundred years. Father has walked this earth for over four hundred years."

"But ... Charlette loves humanity, and she feels their suffering. Did you know she no longer feeds from living humans? Blood-bank cocktails is how she has survived for the past ten years."

"No, I didn't know that, but now that you mention it, I didn't see her feed in Libya, and she did offer me a blood-bank bag, and that was years ago. Wow."

"When you call her, don't talk about me telling you any of this. Wait to see if you can detect the change. Wait to see how she sounds to you. You have to call her with the meeting details, and I am sure Daniel contacted her as he did me."

Daniel communicated with each of us telepathically; initially, I thought it was just me.

"I will. Daniel told me you both were going to the meeting with me."

"Call me after you to speak to her."

"I will."

Juanita just hung up, ending the conversation; she never said goodbye.

I delayed in dialing Charlette's number. The thought of

her feeling cursed by the living-death gave me pause. She did so much good with her existence. All of her wealth went to philanthropic endeavors; she established worldwide charities as opposed to corporations and companies. She fed and cared for humans all across the globe. I didn't want to know what happened to change her attitude. I didn't want to hear her accepting the cursed perspective, especially with my mind set on leaving America. If she, a true world traveler, was feeling discontent, she might have caused me to think that leaving America wasn't enough. That it was all of humanity and not just Americans that were greed filled. I didn't call her.

CHAPTER
- FIVE -

Being burned by the sun had saddened me. I was warned, but the sun had never hurt me until it did. Charlette saved me from total destruction, and she better explained the danger.

"We are fire, and the sun will claim our energy. The less always goes to the greater. When you walk into the sunlight, your energy leaves you – it is simple osmosis. What you are, the energy you have, will join the sun."

We were standing inside the house, and minutes prior she had just dragged me through the patio doors. I stood at the glass patio doors looking out at the family of deer that had tempted me into the sunlight. The deer were still eating the strawberries that Juanita planted.

I had walked into the sun despite being previously told

the sun's beams would destroy me. I saw the family of deer, and I wanted to touch the fawn, so I walked through the patio doors into the sun.

The direct sunlight felt as if it set me ablaze. I couldn't move once I was in the sunlight. All I could do was stand there and disintegrate. Charlette ran outside covered by a tarp; she wrapped me in the tarp with her and dragged me through the patio doors and back into the house.

Inside, away from the direct sunlight, the burns healed instantly. Once I was out of the sun's beams, I was fine. My clothes weren't burned at all; it was just me crumbling to ash.

It took several minutes for me to regain my thoughts. Panic had taken my consciousness. I thought I was doomed.

"I can never walk in the sun?" I finally asked Charlette.

"No, we cannot."

"I really didn't believe it."

"None of us do at first, we all walk into the sun."

I wanted to cry.

"You will learn to love the moonlight and the darkness."

I ignored her words; there was no comparing the moon to the sun, the night to the day.

"We all think that since the daylight barely hurts us, we can walk into the sun."

She extended her brown hand, and I saw it was ashy.

"This looks like ashy skin, but it is the daylight pulling energy from me. My top layers of skin have dried. I only roam the daylight when I must. I advise you to do the same."

She rubbed the back of her hand and I saw the dry skin flake up. I extended my own arms, and they both were ashy. I lowered my hands.

Looking at the fawn that I wanted to touch so badly, I

asked, "Will I ever birth a child?"

Charlette exhaled a long breath. I saw her fingertips touch the glass of the patio door. I heard her inhale and exhale, again.

"We are dead, so we cannot create life, but we can save lives."

We stood at the glass patio door looking out into the daylight and at the family of deer.

"Did you want children?" I asked her.

"No. Shit, I didn't want to be here; there was no way in hell I was going to bring another life into this fucked up world."

I looked from the family of deer to Charlette. I'd never heard anyone sound so final in a decision. The world had problems, I agreed wholeheartedly, but enough not to procreate – that seemed drastic. I would have had children with Christopher. I asked her, "What was so fucked up?"

I saw her deciding if she would answer. Her hand went to her neck and her index finger and thumb rubbed beneath her chin.

"People, and they are still fucked up. But with this living-death, I can make a difference. There is power in living this long."

"How old are you?"

"Me," she laughed and looked from the deer to me. "Well, I'm not older than black pepper, but I am too young to stop caring about people."

That wasn't an answer.

"So, you care for the evil?"

"No, I care for those that fall victim to the deeds of the evil. They need my help, and their need keeps me going, keeps me on this earth."

- Wednesday -

I shuttered my wooden blinds at sunrise and continued to work. I took advantage of Castillo's death and went after some of his shipping company's business. It was easy enough with his death going public the day before. His freight companies were being attacked from all angles, and I joined the feeding frenzy. Expanding into Cuba had been on our "to-do" board for a while; we moved from planning into reality that morning. I had ignored the first call from Marcus when the Cuban manufacture got on board. Three hours later he called back.

"So, you are doing MAM Inc. work today." He had a very light voice that matched his slight stature. We were the same height, and I might have outweighed him by fifteen pounds. MAM Inc. stood for Melody and Marcus Incorporated.

"I'm always doing MAM Inc. work, as I know you are." I was still online and on three screens while talking to him.

"Yeah, well if I'm not flying, I'm buying."

"Buying?"

"Yep, two freight companies, three planes a piece, they were subsidies of Legacy Airlines; one in Brazil, the other in Chile; both are single owner operations."

"When do you close?"

"Closed ... fifteen minutes ago."

We never second-guessed each other because neither of us could make a mistake that could destroy the company; we were richer than God, and we kept getting richer.

"The Cuba move looks good," he said. I heard his keyboard clicking.

"And they want into Africa. Tina Adomako already has

them set up in Ghana and Togo."

"Lumber, right?"

"Yep, and doors and furniture."

"How is Ms. Adomako?"

He'd made the mistake of calling her Tina on their first meeting; he thought them both being my minions made them friends and equals. She immediately corrected him, telling him that she had children his age and the proper respect was expected.

"She is happy and prospering, building a new home."

"Good. Are we still on for seven?"

"Yes, I answered your email."

I felt him before I heard him; it was Reginald, my son. The last person I gave the living-death to.

"I haven't opened that account, sorry," Marcus answered. "Ok, see you tonight."

"Tonight."

Reginald was in pain, a lot of it.

"Mother, open your door." He whimpered inside my head.

I darted to the front door and opened it. He was a dim gaseous ball. I scooped him and brought him inside my condo. He didn't have enough energy to transform. I took him into the kitchen and placed him on the floor. I had bags of plasma in the refrigerator; I opened two and poured them over the gaseous ball that was my son. It was enough. He began to transform.

He dwarfed my five-foot-seven-inch frame. Reginald stood six feet six inches tall. He bent and his hands quickly went to the countertop of the center island for support.

"They almost killed me, Ma. It was a human cop with slayers. They came into my home through my windows, ripping down curtains and blinds and infesting the room with sunlight. They surrounded me on the couch. I was lying on my .45 and my .9mm. I wanted to hear what they wanted before I killed them."

No words were being verbally spoken between my son and me. We were speaking in each other's mind.

"Did the cop have gray and black twists in his hair?"

"Yes, and he knew you too. He said my death would be a warning to you. More slayers came in, and it was apparent they were there to kill me. They started slinging their swords, and I started firing rounds. I was good as long as I avoided the sunbeams, which they knew, so they started directing me toward the sun. They tried to horseshoe me in, with the cop advancing while firing rounds. I killed a couple of them, but my clips emptied, so I swooshed over to the floor vent and took vents down to the basement. I swooshed to the sink pipes and then into the sewers. I made it from Hyde Park to here underground. When I got downtown, I had to come up. I had to swoosh through some sunlight, which got me weak. I barely made it to your door."

I spoke our first words. "Had you seen the cop before?" He chose to answer without speaking, "No, and no slayers had bothered me at home either. The place has been safe for five years, but I have been hearing complaints from other vampires in the city; slayer attacks are increasing in number; something is going on." He looked down at his nakedness. "Do you have any clothes for me?"

"Yes, in the master bath closet; the second shelf is still yours."

He left the kitchen, and I stood there thinking. He was right. Something was going on in the city. The attack on me at the deli supported his claim, and I had never known the local police to work with slayers. I reached out to Daniel and instantly felt him.

"Where are you?"

"Savannah."

"What are you hearing about the slayers here in Chicago?"

"You are correct to worry; there is something happening with the CIA and slayers across America."

"The CIA?"

"Yes, I believe they are being swayed against us. I have to leave you; be careful when you meet with them. I will see you soon, maybe before the meeting." And he was gone from my thoughts.

When I walked into the living room, Reginald was dressed and sitting on my yellow leather sofa with the remote in his hand. The news played on my wall-mounted sixty-inch screen.

I sat on the couch with my son, and after several moments I became annoyed with him because he sat there in new size 17 Adidas gym shoes, which were no easy task to find, and a new custom-made Adidas sweatsuit without uttering a simple thank you ... as if clothes to fit his giant ass were falling off of trees. Finding and keeping clothes for him was not an easy task, but no appreciation seemed forthcoming.

I sat looking at his oversized head with dark brown cornrow braids going to the back ... waiting, but no "thank you" was uttered. If not for his nappy hair, Reginald could be easily mistaken for a white man. He wore his hair in a short afro most of the time. I was just about to comment on his ungratefulness when my mobile and desk phones began ringing at the same time. The fire alarm in the building also sounded. I quickly got up and moved to my office. The screen on the desk phone read "security desk."

I picked it up and heard, "Police and slayers have entered the building. They're coming up the stairs, and they are on the roof." The line clicked dead. It was Jocelyn Warren.

The living room windows shattered, and my blinds were destroyed. Two military dressed officers swung through the window frames. The front door was rammed open, and slayers and uniformed police charged in. My son and I stood from the couch unarmed. If we fled fast enough, nagging bullet tears would be avoided, and we fled fast enough.

We went up across the ceiling because humans never considered the ceiling an escape route. We were gaseous in less than two seconds. Sunbeams had filled the room beneath us; the only out was the return air duct above the front door. We took it.

Jocelyn had warned me against the roof, and the direct sunlight posed too big of a risk. When the vent ducts turned down, we descended, and a blinking light was ahead. I went to it, and we came out in the building's gym. We transformed from gas to two naked vampires in a gym. Jocelyn was there holding a flashlight.

"I pointed the light in the vent. I wasn't sure you would see it. Follow me."

I wasn't afraid of her, but I didn't trust her either; however, our options were limited, so we followed her. She opened what I had thought was a janitor's closet. It was a studio apartment. I thought only the pool and the gym were on the fifth floor.

There were no windows in the tiny apartment, but the wall facing us had a huge framed photograph of the sun setting in the Arabian desert in Iraq. Reginald walked to the photo and stood naked in front of it.

"I've been there. In that same spot. This was taken in Iraq, in the spring."

Jocelyn walked to him and the photo and stood next to my son. "Damn, you are good. I took that the night I shipped home, May 3rd, 2009." They stood side by side looking at the enlarged picture.

Then there was a hard knock at the door. Jocelyn nodded toward the bathroom, and we went straight to it, pulling the door closed behind us.

As soon as I heard his tenor almost bass voice, I knew it was Detective Moss.

"Why did you leave the security desk?"

"I don't work the desk. I was there waiting for coverage; when the guard showed, I left. Why are you asking?"

"Because when we came down from serving the warrant you were gone. I was just curious. Do you mind if I come in?"

"Did your warrant include my home?"

"Should it have?"

"Did it?"

"No."

"Then I see no reason for you to enter."

"I smell her on you. She is a demon. Why would you help her?"

"I have no idea who or what you are talking about."

I heard the front door close.

CHAPTER

- SIX -

"It does hurt," Juanita said, "a lot at first."

Days after I almost disintegrated on the patio, Daniel decided it was time I learned how to "move" as he called it.

"I don't understand how happens, but this is how you do it." She stared at me hard to see if I was listening.

I was. I hadn't forgotten her sternness when teaching.

We were in the den of the house. The large room had patio doors; our backs were against the glass doors.

"Daniel only had to show me once; it took Charlette almost a month to get it. I got it so fast because I saw a vampire die. Another vampire ran a wood spike through his heart."

Her eyes were no longer on me, so I released the breath I was holding. "That works?" I asked, surprised. The only thing I had seen hurt vampires was the sun.

She turned her gaze back to me. "Like magic, I have seen vampires shot in the heart and head, and they kept on moving. But that wooden spike, there is no surviving it."

She grinned at me, and that made me ready to leave her company. "Back to my story, the vampire who died had given the gift to the killer vampire's wife. She had asked her husband, the killer, to give her the gift, but he refused. I guess he didn't want to spend hundreds of years with her. I really don't know why the husband didn't give her the gift, but he stabbed the vampire that did give it to her in the heart with that javelin-like thing. It was wood and once it touched the other vampire's heart, he puffed into a gaseous ball that dissipated into the air. The gas ball didn't have a direction; it was there ... then it wasn't."

I had questions, and if Charlette was telling the story, I would have asked. But I wanted Juanita to complete the lesson so I could leave. Being alone with her bothered me because I was afraid of her.

All Juanita was wearing was a bikini. I had on basketball shorts and a white T. She was looking across the large room to a blue cot with white legs that sat on black tiles that had gold Gye Nyame symbols carved into them.

"You see, when I saw how gas preceded the death of a vampire, and I thought about the pain associated with swooshing, I decided to think about death. I visualized myself dead at the spot I wanted to transform or swoosh or move to. Everybody says swoosh except vampires as old as Daniel. Anyway, so yeah, I saw myself dead on the other side of the room, and bang! I swooshed there. That was how I did it at first until I got good enough to see myself moving as gas."

She looked at me, waiting for a comment.

I had nothing to say. Vampires killing vampires and visualizing death; it was all a bit much.

"Watch," she said with her eyes on the cot.

She swooshed across the room, leaving her bikini at my feet. She was sitting on the blue cot with her legs crossed in less than a second; it was amazing, and she didn't appear in any discomfort.

"Come on over."

I wanted to move like that, to swoosh across a room. But I couldn't visualize myself dead. I couldn't picture myself not alive, then ... I remembered my wedding day. I saw Christopher and his groomsmen bloody. My wedding day, my fiancé, my God. I imagined a death that could have happened. I imagined being shot down and killed on my wedding day. I closed my eyes and saw my bloody corpse in my wedding gown at Juanita's feet.

The pain that tore through me felt as if my body was being forced through a cheese grater; a force was pushing me through. A hand was at my back forcing me through the grates. When I got to Juanita's feet, I was mentally shredded.

"Well done." Daniel was in my head.

"Never again," I said and tearlessly wept at Juanita's feet.

"Get your ass up, it didn't hurt that bad – all that fucking whimpering and shit. Get up! We got to go back."

The second time was no less painful, but the third was, and the fourth was a lot less. Juanita allowed me to dress after the sixth.

"You see, my way doesn't take a month. In a little while, you will be swooshing across the city."

- Wednesday night -

I didn't know how or why they got together, but I was pulled from my resting by the sounds Reginald and Jocelyn made in the bathroom. Before I closed my eyes, I had heard them talking about Iraq. Then, I heard an argument about women soldiers followed by silence. I figured they tired of debating, so I stopped listening until I heard skin smacking into to skin.

I got up and peeped through the cracked bathroom door, and there was nothing romantic about what I witnessed. Jocelyn was on all fours and Reginald was on his knees behind her. They looked like two polar bears mating. I tiptoed back to the couch. A short while later Jocelyn surfaced first, naked.

I asked her, "Are the police still on the rooftop?"

She answered, "No, the guards tell me one detective unit is parked in front of the building, and two slayers are circling the block in a jeep, and four more are in the building still searching, but no one is on the roof." She glanced over the room and located her clothes on the floor in front of the kitchen counter. She went to them.

Reginald walked from the bathroom to a kitchen stool and sat at the counter. He avoided my glance.

Jocelyn said, "I think it is safe enough for me to go get you guys clothes."

I picked up her landline phone and dialed Marcus's number. He answered on the second ring.

"I'm here ... waiting on you." He was at the airport waiting to show me the chopper.

"There has been a change in plans; come get me and two guests from my building. And don't change the flight plan, I don't want to attract any attention; we are going to have to pay the fine."

I asked the kitchen, "Two?" I was making the assumption that Jocelyn was going with us. I might have been wrong.

Jocelyn answered, "Yes, two."

"Ok ... you plus two." Marcus had landed the chopper on the roof before, so him coming to us should not have been a problem, but I heard hesitation in his confirmation.

"You haven't seen the news, have you?" he asked.

"No."

"Then you don't know."

"Marcus, what is it?"

"Your friend, your group leader, Daniel, he died. Their plane exploded. It was your friend, a senator from Ohio, and a congressman from Georgia. The news referred to your friend as a corporate executive traveling with the senator."

"What are you talking about?"

I immediately tried to reach out to Daniel, and for the first time in thirty-seven years, I felt nothing.

I told Marcus, "Be here in twenty minutes," and hung up.

Reginald heard the conversation and asked me verbally, "What do you think?" He sounded like a concerned child. Daniel had been a mentor to him.

"I can't reach him. I have never not felt him. I don't know." My legs gave way, and I collapsed by the phone, but Reginald caught me before I got to the carpet and sat me on the couch.

It felt like I had been kicked in my stomach.

"I need my computer."

Jocelyn was dressed and said, "I can go get it, no

problem. You guys stay here."

She had barely opened the door when the slayers broke into the apartment. If there was ever a wrong time and a wrong place, those two blind slayers were in it. The uncertainty I felt changed to focused annihilation, and the slayers became the recipients of that destruction.

I beat them to death with my bare hands before either Jocelyn or Reginald could move. I had to, each blow to a temple was a search, a call out to Daniel. Repeated backhand blows crushing a nose was me reaching for the plane and not finding it. Driving a knee into a lower back while snatching back a head, causing a snap that echoed through the small apartment, was my mind reaching for Savannah, only to find no trace of him. When I used my elbow to crush a larynx, not feeling Daniel was understood. He was gone.

The slayers' deaths were bloodless. I watched the polar bears drag the slayers' corpses into the bathroom.

"Others will be looking for them."

"Yes, but not in your apartment." Jocelyn said, closing the bathroom door. "And if they do come in here, you two can do the gas thing and leave. I will be alright."

Reginald and I needed clothes, and I needed my computer. We took the stairs up and met no resistance. We heard slayers on the floors beneath us; they were working their way down.

My home was wrecked, and my cell phone and computer had been knocked off my desk into the seat of my office chair. The jeweled dagger Daniel gave me when I reached my Oh Dan blackbelt in Taekwondo was resting in its bronze stand undisturbed. I grabbed it, my phone, and my computer with its bag. Reginald and I quickly dressed. We only had minutes; Marcus had to be close, but I had to make a call anyway. I dialed from my desk phone. When the line was picked up, I asked, "Charlette?"

"Hey, Fawn." Her voice was heavy; none of the cheerful airiness I had grown to expect was present. Charlette started calling me Fawn after she saved me from the sun. She only called me Fawn when one of us was hurting.

"Juanita and I were trying to decide who would call you."

"I can't feel him."

Reginald put his arm around my shoulders.

"Because he's gone, Fawn. The bomb tore the jet to pieces, and it blew up in the sunlight. There is no Daniel to feel."

I thought about what she said, and it made sense. He was ripped to shreds by a bomb in the sunlight. There was no Daniel; my father was dead.

Juanita spoke on the line, "And we are going to find out who murdered him."

"Yes," Charlette and I answered.

"And destroy them and their linage, so nothing of them will remain of this earth." Juanita was swearing us to an oath.

"Yes," we both agreed.

Daniel was the head of our family, and he had been murdered. Vampire retribution was family based; if it was a vampire family, we would war until there were none of us left. If it was a human who killed him, that human and his offspring would be drained to dust – and that included slayers.

"Slayers and the Chicago police raided both my and Reginald's homes. Meet us at my home in Gary, Indiana."

"Fawn, pick me up tomorrow from Midway at 8:30

p.m.," Charlette said.

"I will."

Juanita asked, "Is the house code still 1619?"

"Yes, goodbye."

Hurried, I looked to Jocelyn and told her, "Going with us will change your life forever."

She tightened a strap on her form-fitting backpack and said, "Not really. I am a soldier and a gypsy. It was time to leave a year ago."

Reginald tapped on the desk with his knuckles. "Time to go."

We three boldly walked into the hall. There was no fear in our strut. I think each of us was craving battle, but no slayers or police were in the hall or stairwell.

The roof was big enough, but the wind from the chopper's blades bent the phone tower and the TV antennas over. The high wind presented a challenge, but we loaded quickly. Neither of the polar bears fit easily into the back of the chopper. They were adjusting against each other for space that wasn't there. Once in, we all put on the headsets.

"Good to see you, man," Marcus greeted Reginald.

"You too, bro. Still getting rich with Ma, I see. New chopper?"

"It is. We brought it last week. And greetings to you, young lady. I am Marcus Lane, Melody's business partner and pilot."

Jocelyn was still adjusting in the tight space. "Nice to meet you, Mr. Lane. I am Jocelyn Warren – not sure of my designation yet, so let's go with soldier for hire."

Her answer caused Marcus to look at me. "Really? Who hired you, Melody or Reginald?"

She settled in the seat by placing a leg across my son's

thigh. "Reginald pulled me in, but I think Melody will pay my fees."

Marcus and I closed the chopper doors. "That sounds about right, buckle up."

I heard their chatter, but I was not in the mood for small talk. A bomb, Charlette said a bomb blew up the plane.

"What more did you hear on the news?" was my question to Marcus.

He had the helicopter airborne; he gave me a quick look then targeted his eyes out the front window of the helicopter into the blue sky.

"It was a 737. They are searching for the black box, not survivors. The explosion sent pieces of the jet across Georgia. There are over five crash site locations so far."

"Did they say anything about a bomb?"

Again, he looked at me briefly then back to the night sky.

"No, but jet explosions happen in engines, leaving parts of the plane, so for there to be only debris indicates a powerful explosion or multiple explosions."

"He was murdered," I confirmed for myself.

Looking down at my phone, I entered Chad Oliver, my CIA handler's number.

I texted, "Meet me tonight, in Gary."

He answered, "After eight?"

I answered, "Yes" and stopped texting. Whatever he knew, he would tell me, one way or another. It was Daniel that kept my relationship with the CIA civil. With him gone, my actions would be mine.

"Natalie," my thoughts went out to my daughter.

She answered, "Yes, Mother," and I was relieved.

"I am expecting guests at the house."

"Here in Gary?"

"Yes, and I want you there. Juanita may beat us there, and so may Chad Oliver."

"Us?"

"Your brother, Marcus, and a friend of your brother's is traveling with us."

"Reginald doesn't have any friends, Ma, but ok."

"There is danger, be alert."

"I saw the news. I know about Daniel."

She was not close to him, and her distance had nothing to do with my father; Natalie hated most men.

"His death is only part of the danger," I told her.

"Ok, Mother, I understand."

We released each other's thoughts.

No one else in the chopper spoke until Reginald asked, "What happens with Daniel?"

I was not sure what he was asking. I offered, "Charlette, Juanita, and I will divide his estate in thirds."

"No, I'm asking about the oath you and the others took. What happens with that with the retribution? I am not sure I understand."

I had never discussed vampire duties with either of my children until the lesson needed to be taught, which was how Daniel raised me. I adjusted the seatbelt and said, "Daniel was the head of my family. Ours is a small family, so we three – Charlette, Juanita, and I – are bound to avenge his death, and we will."

"Who or what binds you?"

"Tradition and the other families. If we do not act, Daniel's memory would be disgraced, and we would have no claim to his estate. As you know, most of vampires' wealth is managed by other vampires because our wealth is worldwide, and we live for centuries.

"We must manage our own wealth; the vastness and the time is beyond human comprehension. We operate in centuries; humans barely manage decades. Daniel was part of a family when he started our family. Wealth from the family he was part of was passed onto him. The third I will receive from Daniel's estate will become part of my wealth. Upon my demise, you and Natalie will divide my wealth; if my destruction is caused by another, tradition will require the two of you to go to war. If you fail to balance the injustice, my reputation and this family's name is disgraced among vampires."

He nodded his head in understanding.

"Would we still get your wealth if we don't act?"

"It is doubtful because you will be seen as weak. Others will take what you have been left."

"I understand. That is why I am Reginald Knight and no longer Thaddeus Blakes."

"Correct you are, my son."

CHAPTER
- SEVEN -

The first person I gave the living-death to was a young woman praying for another's damnation. I was in Philadelphia on business, and not planning on feeding, but the scent of despair was so strong, I was drawn to another hotel suite. When I entered the bedroom, a young woman was standing over a man with a bloody butcher's knife in hand. The knife was dripping blood onto the stomach of a still living Black male in his early thirties. I transformed from gas to woman.

The young woman holding the knife was not frightened by my transformation. She looked from me back to the man in the bed, and repeatedly plunged the butcher's knife down. The knife was not going into the man's stomach, but into his genital area.

After several stabs, she stopped and stepped back.

"You can take his soul now," she said to me.

"What?" I asked.

"You are the Angel of Death, right? You are here for his soul. God answered my prayers and he sent you. He is going to burn in hell for raping and killing my sister. And I know I will be there with him ... but burning in hell for eternity is ok with me. I got his ass."

Looking down at the man, I saw that he was close to bleeding to death. She had destroyed his genitals, and blood was pumping from his thigh onto the mattress.

Her head turned to a questioning angle. "Or are you here for my soul?" she asked, putting the butcher's knife to her wrist. I was on her before she could slice it. I took her to near death and stopped.

Daniel told me I would instinctively know when the living-death should be given. I wanted to give it to the young woman. I laid her on the floor at the foot of the bed. I reached out to Daniel.

"Yes, Melody?"

"I need help. I want to bring this young lady home."

"Ah, your first child. Where are you?"

"Philadelphia."

"Stay with your child. Alexander and I will be there shortly."

When they arrived, Alexander placed the young unconscious woman into a wheelchair. He covered her with a blanket, then pushed her from the hotel to the waiting limo. Daniel held me behind in the room.

"Why her?" he asked me.

"She is grief stricken and ready to die; that thing in the bed raped and killed her sister. She killed him and was ready

to die and spend eternity in hell. If I had not been here, she would have killed herself. She had settled on eternity in hell, so I am offering her something more."

"What if she doesn't want it?"

"Then she can walk into the sun, hell, I don't know. I just gave her what you gave me when I was in that state, a choice. It seemed like the right thing to do."

My father placed his arm across my shoulders. "It was, Melody. It was the right thing to do. She will be the first in your family. Soon, it will be time for you to move into your own home and start another Knight family."

- Wednesday night -

My home in Gary was on the lakefront, a one-level brick ranch. It was my first home, and it was where I started my family with Natalie. Chad walked in that night dressed in blue jeans, a yellow Izod, and white deck shoes, and as soon as I saw him, I was certain he knew something about Daniel's death.

He would not maintain eye contact with Juanita or me. Reginald had opened the front door for him, so he walked into a living room filled with vampires: Reginald, me, Natalie, and Juanita. Marcus and Jocelyn were in the kitchen eating a pizza.

"You smell scared," Reginald whispered to him, closing the front door.

Chad tried to laugh the words off, but the well-lit room showed the perspiration forming on his forehead. Natalie liked track lights and chandeliers, and she had both installed in the living room.

"No, I'm just a little tired. It has been a long day."

Towering over him, Reginald contradicted Chad with, "No, that is fear I smell. Please, go on in – we don't bite."

The "we don't bite" comment broke Natalie out in laughter. She stood up from the eggshell white French provincial settee that was next to fireplace. "Why did you lie to that man like that, of course we bite." She turned her eyes fire red and brought her canines forward; that stopped Chad's advancement into the living area. Natalie moved across the room like a comet and stood face to face with him. Reginald, still standing behind him, heavily placed his huge hands on Chad's shoulders.

Neither I nor Juanita spoke. Chad had worked with us in the past; he knew us. He had never worked with Natalie or Reginald. I decided to leave getting the truth from him ... to them. In their minds, I told them both, "He is all yours."

Natalie turned her head to me and smiled; she looked back at Chad and stated, "My mother's father was murdered. I never liked him, but I don't like most men, and I hate all human men. All I feed on is human men, so honestly, you are smelling like dinner to me." She was sniffing under his chin and at his neck. "Yeah, you are smelling really tasty."

Reginald picked Chad up by his shoulders, moving him from Natalie's gaze.

"Naw, sis, don't drain him. This man is Mama's friend. He came to talk to Mama."

Reginald suddenly slung Chad to the floor with extreme force. Chad's gun and phone flew across the hardwood floor. He placed his foot on Chad's chest. "I did like my mother's father, he taught me a lot. So, before my sister drains your ass dry, I'm going to give you one chance to tell my mother and her sister something that impresses them. You got one chance."

Juanita and I stood from the couch and walked over to him. We looked down at him on the floor, and we both turned our eyes red and extended our canines. Chad didn't hesitate to spill the beans.

"The slayers, they placed the bomb. We don't know why, and we are not supposed to know they placed it. We found out through a brief investigation; a plane loader's bank account jumped up fifty thousand dollars after the explosion.

"He was questioned, and he said a man with white eyes paid him fifty thousand cash and promised another fifty thousand into his bank account. He handed over the fifty thousand in cash to the agents that questioned him. We caught him before his shift ended. We – me, the CIA – had nothing to do with Daniel's death."

Hope rang through his hurried oration; he was praying the words would save him.

"The name of the field worker?" Juanita demanded.

"What?" Chad's eyes were moving from vampire to vampire; he didn't know who to fear more.

"The worker who placed the bomb on the plane, his name?" Juanita squatted down to him.

"Lawrence Owens, but he is in custody; the local police have him."

She rose and pulled out her phone and dialed a number. "Charlette, stop in Georgia. Lawrence Owens is in a Savannah jail; he put the bomb on the plane." She hung up.

"Can I get up now?" Chad looked up at me, but I didn't answer him.

"That won't be easy for Charlette," I said, thinking about

Charlette's diet of blood-bank bags, and her current disillusionment with the living-death.

"It's not stopping with Lawrence Owens and his family; slayers were behind the attack. We need him to have that meeting with the slayers." Juanita nodded her head towards Chad. "Let him up." She directed Reginald.

Reginald moved his foot, but he did not offer Chad any assistance from the floor; no one did.

Chad stood dusting himself off and arranging his clothes. Natalie's foot was on top of his phone and pistol. Chad saw her foot and looked to me, pleading. I walked back to the couch and sat down.

"Slayers and the Chicago police raided my son's home and my home. Why?" I wanted more from him.

He exhaled, "I don't know. I thought everything was on hold until the meeting."

Natalie unexpectedly slapped him across his face. "What do you mean, 'everything was on hold'? What the fuck is everything?"

With his eyes gapped wide and his hand on his cheek, he took steps back out of Natalie's reach and said, "Slayer actions in regard to vampires; there is supposed to be some type of common ground involving the CIA, vampires, and slayers. Slayers should not be killing you guys."

Juanita looked at him like he was wearing a dunce cap. "I don't think the slayers got the message. They have been attacking vampires all across the country, and you are telling me the CIA knows nothing?"

Chad stepped further away, rubbing the area of his face Natalie slapped. "I can't speak for slayers across the country, I can only speak for those attempting to work with the CIA."

Juanita ran her fingers through her long black hair,

obviously frustrated with what he was saying. "Why are slayers being brought in to work with the CIA in the first place?"

Chad stopped rubbing his cheek and put both of his hands into the front pockets of his jeans. "For a balance of power; honestly, the agency has identified a vulnerability in working with vampires. Vampire goals are being met over agency concerns; for example, Fernando Castillo." He looked directly at me. "We wanted him alive, but Melody, you wanted him dead, and he is dead. A vampire's goal was placed over the agency's; the hope is that slayer involvement will leave the agency less dependent on vampires; we are hoping for more team players."

Natalie laughed out loud, and she targeted her outbreak at Chad. "Ok, you know that slayers exist only to kill vampires, right?" She walked up next to Juanita. "Their whole existence is for our destruction; we are why they exist. You know that, right?" She snapped the "right" at him, and he flinched at the word.

Chad took more steps back; he was almost against the wall-mounted television. "I know that is how it was, but the hope is that the CIA will bring the two groups together for the benefit of America."

Juanita came to me, but she didn't sit next to me on the couch; she chose the easy chair. "While they are still attacking us?"

Chad blinked his eyes several times, but he didn't answer her. I could tell he was looking for a route away from Natalie.

"What do you know about Detectives Moss and Bowman?" was my query.

"Who?'

"Two Chicago police detectives, Moss and Bowman," I added for clarification.

"I don't know either name."

"That's a lie." Jocelyn and Marcus had entered the living area. "I saw you talking to Detective Moss right before he and slayers invaded our building. You were right there with the slayers and the police. You didn't come into the building, but you were there," Jocelyn challenged him.

Chad's eyes went to his pistol, still under Natalie's foot. It was an admission of guilt. All I saw were the straight black strands of Juanita's hair zoom past me. She didn't kill him, but she beat him to compliance.

He was back on the hardwood floor with a bloody nose, and I guessed several cracked ribs. Juanita was tired of playing with him. "What are you doing with the slayers? Tell me about Friday's meeting."

Reginald walked to him and placed a foot on his chest. He leaned forward, applying weight.

Chad released, "It's a trap. The slayers want the Knight family destroyed."

Chad's words obviously shocked Juanita; she looked down at him perplexed. "Our family? Why our family?"

Reginald leaned forward, putting more weight on Chad's chest.

"I don't have a fucking clue, but my bosses agreed that your family was a major threat. And Detective Moss said he could get it done before Friday with the help of the slayers, so I agreed."

I wanted him to state it plainly.

"You agreed to kill us? You agreed to kill me, Daniel, Juanita, and Charlette. People who have been working with you your entire career? You agreed to kill us?"

He groaned and Reginald removed his foot, but he continued to stand over him.

Chad rolled from being flat on his back to his side.

"I was following orders, which is what agents do. Vampires are shitty agents, ok. And the powers-that-be want you all gone. But you vampires are in too deep, you guys have history with the agency, you are too well informed. The administration believes firing all the vampires has too many estimated calamities. The compromised positions and damages are through the roof. Just severing ties won't work. The agency wants you all eradicated, and the slayers claim they can deliver.

"The local police across the country are uninformed about what you are; nobody fucking believes in vampires. Local cops and the FBI are just following orders; orders from slayers and us; we generate the target list."

"We who – the CIA and slayers?" Juanita was trembling with anger. "We have worked with the CIA since its inception, why now?"

Chad sat up and looked at Juanita like she was a student. "Your kind doesn't follow orders, and you are in too deep to fire. The slayers offered a solution, and the directors took it."

"Slayers," every vampire in the room said.

"We need that meeting," Natalie calculated.

I added, "We need Detective Moss."

"Why do we need the meeting?" Reginald asked, stepping on Chad's thigh and causing him to wail out in pain as the vampire kept walking to his sister.

"To get some top slayers," Natalie answered.

"No such thing, they are all blind drones that follow orders," Marcus joined.

Reginald shook his head no. "Somebody planned something, somebody paid the airport worker, somebody convinced the CIA to turn against us, and somebody told them to target our family. So, we go the meeting, and we kidnap some slayers. It becomes our trap instead of theirs."

Juanita kicked Chad hard in his broken ribs, and he cried out again in pain and collapsed back on the hardwood floor. "Looks like we need you alive, at least for now," my sister told him.

CHAPTER
- EIGHT -

She woke in the same room I woke in when Daniel gave me
the living-death. And I sat at the same table where Daniel
had sat with a lit candle. When she stood, she immediately
focused on me.

"Where am I?"

"In my home."

"Where?"

"Chicago."

"I didn't die?"

"You did, but you were given a different life."

"You bit me."

"I did."

"You are not the Angel of Death."

"No, I am not."

"You are a vampire," she accused. "You are not from God."

"I don't know that."

I believed in God, but my thinking had not advanced to the point of considering God's relationship with vampires.

"A vampire," she confirmed.

"I am, and now ... so are you."

She looked down at Daniel's bed, but her mind was not in that room.

"He raped my eight-year-old sister. We were homeless, but we were doing ok. I gave him some pussy to stay in his basement. I fucked him every day to stay there. The day I went down to the aide office, he raped her and murdered her. When I got back, she was dead; the police were there. He told them someone must have broken in the house while he was at work. They believed him, but I didn't. I knew he did it. I walked the streets for three weeks, hoping in and out of cars hoeing. Then this white boy gave me these pills that knock people out. He said I just had to open one and pour it into a drink. I went back to his house. I told him I needed a shower, and that I needed him to rent me a room. I showered and walked in front of him naked. If he saw my titties, he would do whatever I wanted. He always did. He rented me the room. I opened two pills and poured them into his beer. They didn't knock him out, but they wouldn't let him move. He was face down in the bed grunting, so I rolled him over. His eyes were moving but nothing else; he couldn't even talk, only grunt. I slapped the shit out him. His eyes opened wide. He knew what was going to happen. Then I started praying. Talking to God right in front of him. Praying that the Lord put his soul in Hell, and I prayed to God to send the Angel of Death, so I could see him take his soul. I started stabbing him *in his dick and balls, then you appeared, right in front of me. I was ready to die. My sister was all that was left of the life we had when we had parents. Then he killed her, and all that was left was hoeing and being homeless. With my sister, I thought God would make things better because she was innocent. She still believed in Santa Claus, and with her, I believed things would get better. People did things for her: the shelter workers would always let us in, the grocery store workers always brought us out food, and the lady at the aide office had worked it out so we would be in the same foster care home. People did stuff for her, and God liked her, but he killed her, and God took her, and He left me by myself. I was ready to die. But you bit me, and I am still alive."*

- Wednesday -

Natalie and I shared the bed in the master bedroom, but we didn't rest. We lay on the pillows looking up at freshly painted ceilings. She took good care of the home; there was no arguing that.

"I smelled her all over him."

She was talking about Reginald and Jocelyn. They had taken a room together.

As a big sister, as a guide, as a teacher, Natalie had been excellent with Reginald, but she consistently found fault in most of his actions.

I fluffed my pillow and adjusted my head. I was not planning on sitting up. I really wanted my mind to slow down, so I closed my eyes while we talked. She remained sitting up, and I felt her looking down at me.

"He thinks with his penis."

"That's not true."

It was partially true; eighty percent of Reginald's problems stemmed from his relationships with women, vampire and human.

"Everyone does not think and plan simultaneously as you do. Some of us react before thinking things through. Why are you always so hard on your brother?"

"Because he refuses to stop and think and to plan. Two months ago, I asked him to help me paint the inside of this house. He refused because he said we had the money to pay painters. I wanted to talk to him about going into business with me; I needed a male speaker, and he has a compelling story, but due to him refusing to help me paint, we never talked."

"You did the painting?"

"No, I hired painters. The youngest Shore brother, Jessie, has a remolding company."

"You could have just told your brother what you actually wanted."

"No, I can never ask him for help straight out. Me requesting his help gives him too much pleasure. He really has a little brother-big sister thing going on with me."

I opened my eyes and looked up at her. "What does that mean? I am little sister to Charlette and Juanita, and there are times when they ask me for assistance."

"But you are a little sister, not a younger brother. Reginald is resentful because I am a woman who knows more than him."

"My sisters were better informed than me. They trained me; a bit brutal at times, but that doesn't stop us from helping each other. Older siblings train younger siblings."

She exhaled heavily and looked down at me like I was

confused. "I understand that, but Reginald only followed my advice because he had to. I taught him how to feed, how to swoosh, how to move in the daylight, and he has always been bitter because it was me teaching him. Me, a woman, teaching him, a man."

"But why?"

"Because he is a man, and I am a woman, and I was the boss of him, and he knew he would not have survived without my guidance, and that annoyed him. He believes men should lead women."

"Still, really?" I thought he had changed some of his superior male beliefs.

"Yes, really." She looked annoyed, like I had missed the obvious.

"I find it hard to believe that he is still that small-minded."

Natalie had a problem with men.

"Believe it, Mother. Reginald is a pig."

I was motherly and asked, "And none of the hostility between you two starts with you?"

She threw the cover from her legs and swung them around to the side of the bed and placed her feet soundly on the carpeted floor. I watched her slender shoulders rise and fall as she breathed.

"I admittedly have issues with men."

I raised my head again and fluffed my pillow. Wanting to change the subject, I said, "Except for Nelson Shore."

She quickly twisted her head to face me.

"What?"

"Nelson Shore, you don't seem to have issues with him."

She laid her head back down on her pillow and faced me.

"Well, Mother, that is because he is gorgeous. Oh my God, he is so fine. I could look at him for days. Well, I have looked at him for days."

"Yes, so I've heard."

"From who?"

"From the television; I saw you two in France at the Janet Jackson concert."

"He flew me there in his private jet."

She was grinning literally from ear to ear.

"Are you in the mile-high club?"

Her eyes blinked rapidly. "What?" She kept smiling. "Oh Mother, please."

She didn't like to talk about sex – at least not with me. "I'm just curious; it took me two years after I was given the gift to have sex. I wish I would not have waited so long, that's all."

Her lips stopped smiling, but her eyes were still bright and cheerful.

"Yes, well that is not my story, Mother."

"Or your brother's either, apparently. You both are fucking like bunnies."

"Mother, come on, please, can we change the subject?"

She looked from me to the ceiling.

"Ok ... ride with me and Juanita to get Charlette."

"Yes, of course."

The knock on the bedroom door was rapid and hard.

"Yes," I answered.

"We might be losing that CIA guy, come quick." Marcus beckoned.

We both stood from the bed and made it out into the living area then into the kitchen. Chad had been stretched out atop the kitchen table. He was unconscious and laboring for breath.

Juanita spoke first. "How bad do we need him?"

"The meeting is at the CIA offices downtown; I guess we could show up without him," was my answer.

"Yeah, but his phone has rung twice in the last hour." Reginald sounded worried. "They might be looking for him."

"We don't know who he told he was coming see us." Natalie was standing next to me, looking down at Chad.

Juanita was taking his pulse, and she thumbed open his eyelids and asked, "Anybody want a CIA minion?"

"No," my children answered almost in unison.

"Then should we give him the living-death?" I asked everyone at the table.

"No," was the harmonious answer.

I told them, "But we need to heal him for our meeting plans to work. Either we take him to a human hospital, make him a minion, or give him the gift." In response to my ultimatum, the group's stare was on me.

Juanita said, "We can't take him to a hospital; he will certainly talk to people and our plans will be blown. Someone has to make him a minion – that's the only safe way to save his life."

For some reason, they were all still looking at me.

"Why me?"

"You have minions," Juanita answered, "none of us have done it before."

"But you all know how it is done. Substitute the blood you take with yours; it is a very simple process. What's going on here ... is that none of you want the intimacy, and the responsibility of this man as a minion. So, what makes you think I do?"

I turned away from the table, Chad, and them. I was about to walk away when Marcus spoke.

"You gave me this power at my request, and I have never forgotten it can be taken as easily as you gave it to me. So, I do the best I can with it every day. I have not forgotten how I was living when I begged you for the power. I have not forgotten the person I was. But this power has changed me. The responsibility you spoke of ... is on the minion as well. I can break any human's neck. I can hear a conversation a block away or behind a board room door. I process information at a speed people can only dream of.

"With these advantages came responsibility. The man I was would probably try to rule the world with the power. The man I have become because of the power cares about the world and knows ruling is only a fantasy of the greedy. What I am trying to say is that if you make this man a minion ... what he was will change. Your blood does more than empower us; it changes our thinking. This man will change for the better; that's just how it works."

Turning to face them all, I said "But I don't like him."

"Ooh my God!" came from Marcus. He stood erect with his eyes roaming.

With her eyes wide, Juanita whispered, "They are surrounding us."

"I hear a lot of them," Natalie said.

"Swoosh to the lake and use the boat. Jocelyn, follow Marcus. He will get you there." I was talking and transforming at the same time.

We were gaseous and gone before they attacked.

From the boat, we watched the Gary city police and slayers raid my home. The darkness allowed Marcus and Jocelyn to leave through a back window without a shot being fired. We didn't start the boat even when Marcus and Jocelyn made it to the water and boarded.

We all sat quiet in Daniel's eight passenger Sea Ray, watching. I looked to Marcus and saw he had grabbed my laptop and my phone from the house. He was indeed a good minion.

Ambulance attendants went into the house. Slayers with nocturnal vison gear began circling the outside of the house, but neither they nor the police seemed willing to come through the wooded area to the lake. I was worried about them finding the chopper and wrecking it, but none came into the woods. The attendants brought Chad out covered with a sheet. He was dead.

Detective Moss stood in my front porch light watching them load Chad's covered corpse in the back of the ambulance. He had my dagger, the one Danial gave me, in his hand.

I started the boat and told Marcus to call Alexander.

He pulled his phone from his pocket and made the call. "We are on our way. Yes, from the dock."

Daniel taught each of us how to drive the boat after he and Alexander built the dock at my house. Going from dock to dock at night took skill, and it was a trip we often made. The boat was fast, and I needed to feel its speed. I full throttled across the dark water under the star-filled sky. I felt the others wanting me to slow down, but I didn't, and they all sat quiet.

CHAPTER
- NINE -

We – Charlette, Alexander, and I – had taken Natalie out for her first feeding. As I expected, she was not the least bit timid concerning the kill, and she was neat as a pin throughout the whole process. She drained the man dry without losing a drop.

The man was forcing a male prostitute to accept a meager amount at gunpoint. Natalie followed the lust-heavy scent down the stairs of a garden apartment where the transaction was occurring. The aggressor was standing above the kneeled prostitute with his penis in the prostitute's mouth and his pistol to the prostitute's head.

Natalie moved quickly. She snatched the aggressor's head back and to the left and sunk in her canines, all in one movement. She drained him with his penis still in the prostitute's mouth. The aggressor deflated and Natalie went down with him. She fed until there was only skin and dry bones remaining. The kneeling prostitute observed it all with unexpected calm.

"Vampires," he said, looking at Natalie then at me. "You need helpers, right? And you exchange wealth for the help, right?"

I answered, "Yes." He had bright emerald green eyes and fire red hair. I doubted that he weighed a hundred and five pounds wet.

With no fear, the prostitute said, "I need a job, urgently." He was still on his knees.

His fearlessness and his knowledge impressed me.

"How do you know about our kind?"

"Movies, and she is drinking his blood." *He nodded his head toward a still feeding Natalie.*

I couldn't help but laugh.

"Please, I need help," *he said with no humor in his voice. What I heard and smelled was desperation.*

"I could use a minion, but you must be intelligent."

He remained on his knees, "I have a BS in accounting and an MBA."

"The minion process is painful."

"My life is painful." *He picked up the aggressor's gun and stood. He put the gun in his back pocket.*

Natalie stood and said, "It reminded me of garlic fried chicken wings." *She looked at the redhead.* "You should go through his wallet." *She nodded toward the corpse.*

Alexander and Charlette appeared on the sidewalk above. "Sunrise in fifteen minutes," *Alexander informed us, looking at his watch.*

Charlette looked at the corpse. "Nowhere near as messy

as your mother's first feeding. Huh, Melody? And what have we here?" she asked, pointing her finger at the prostitute.

I looked at him and asked, "What is your name?"

"Marcus Lane."

"This is Marcus, my minion."

"Ha, ha, ha," Alexander barked, "A minion needs brawn, a strong back, and a fearless heart. He doesn't appear to have any of those."

Marcus was about to protest, but he saw my slight hand gesture and remained silent. I liked that; from the start, before I bit him, he was able to follow my intentions.

"You are brawn, Alexander, but not all minions are brawn; please be kind to Marcus."

Alexander's response was a grunt. Daniel's response was a bit more paternal.

We were sitting at his dining room table: Alexander, Juanita, Natalie, Charlette, and myself. Marcus was unconscious on the garage floor; I had drained almost half his body's blood. When he woke, I would feed him a gauntlet of mine.

"Some never pass on the living-death, and others take centuries, and neither is a bad thing. Each vampire takes a different path. You are my youngest daughter, and the first to start a house. The first to extend the Knight clan, and I am not surprised. Your mind seldom rests, and I don't know if that is a good thing, but I knew you would build a house.

"I bought you a home across the lake. It reminds me of you, small but very sturdy. Paul from the Wilson clan assures me it is a good purchase. You are only a boat ride away. Alexander will drive you across the lake tonight."

Vampires don't shed tears, but Charlette, Juanita, and I were choked up. And Daniel must have been too because he abruptly stood from the table saying, "I have a meeting. Alexander, I am taking the Benz. I won't need you tonight."

Before he could leave, I asked, "Wait, are you kicking me out?" I fully understood what he was doing, but I wasn't ready for him to leave.

"No, these doors are always open to you, but my dear Melody, you have outgrown these walls."

- Thursday -

Being in Daniel's home and not feeling him ... was painful. Not being able to reach out to him, and not hearing him inside my thoughts ... was lonely; an emptiness was in my mind. The space he once occupied was vacant, and accepting that he was gone ... was reality. I sat at his table fully aware that a CIA and slayer attack was looming, but my shoulders were weighed down. All I could do was look at everyone else.

Daniel's kitchen was much larger than mine, so we were all congregated there sitting in chairs and on counter stools. Only Jocelyn was standing; she was at the open refrigerator pulling out a bottle of water.

My phone rang and looking down, I saw Charlette's number. I answered and heard, "It's done. There was only him. He had no wife or children. Where are you and Juanita?"

"We are at Daniel's, planning."

"For what?"

"The attack is larger than we thought. The CIA is attempting to eradicate vampires, and their plan is to start with the Knight clan."

The line was quiet.

"I don't doubt it, but it is stupid. I will meet you all at home, no need to pick me up."

Home, Daniel's place had been our home.

I told her, "Someone will be here when you arrive."

"See you soon," and she hung up.

We all should have been planning something, but we were just sitting. Charlette was the only one actively doing something; she killed the man that placed the bomb on the plane.

"We need that cop," Reginald said.

"Why?" Marcus asked.

"Because he is always there. Whenever anything happens, his ass is there."

My son was right. Detective Moss was knee deep in the attacks. "He tried to be a slayer, but he couldn't complete the training." I slipped my laptop bag from my shoulder and pulled the computer out. I placed it on the table and flipped it opened. "I have a file on him." While the file was opening, my phone rang again. It was my godson, Thomas.

He didn't wait for a greeting. "Those detectives we spoke of earlier are at my house, and they have threatened to take me to jail unless I contact you."

I stood from chair. "Are they alone?"

"Yes. It appears so."

Thomas was not a minion; he was only human with human fears.

"Give one of them the phone."

I heard them refusing to take the phone.

"We don't need to talk to her. She heard you. Tell her to get her demon ass over here or you are going to jail."

Thomas got back on the phone. "They claim to want to

talk to you about Castillo's murder."

I asked, "Are your wife and children safe?"

"Yes, Tammy is upstairs with the twins."

I told him, "See you soon," and hung up.

They weren't there to arrest Thomas. They were trying to force me into the open, but Moss didn't know we were no longer on the defense. We were on offense, and his demand was exactly what we needed. I put my phone on the kitchen table and sat back down.

"You are not going to believe this, but Detective Moss and his partner are alone at Thomas's house demanding to see me." I didn't address anyone directly. I went back to Moss's file on my laptop.

Natalie stood from her stool. "Well, let's go give them what they want." She walked towards me at the table.

Juanita stood from her chair and started pacing. "No, that doesn't make any sense; why just a Chicago police presence if the attack is a slayer and CIA plan?"

"Maybe the CIA is close by," Marcus offered.

"And the slayers," Jocelyn added.

"Too many enemies; it's sounding like a trap." Reginald spun around on his stool to face me.

Juanita stopped pacing. "Of course it is trap, but they don't know how informed we are."

"Again, there are too many enemies. The CIA wants to eliminate vampires from their operations; to see if it is possible, they are starting with us. Why us first?" Reginald quieted the kitchen with that question.

Alexander stood from his stool and began pacing. I can count on my fingers the times he had spoken without being asked a question.

"There are two enemies: slayers and the CIA. Slayers

have joined forces with the CIA because the CIA wants to end its working relationships with vampires, but they fear repercussions from ending the relationship; is this correct?" Alexander asked.

"Yes," Juanita answered, looking as surprised as I felt at Alexander's words.

"Is there any way to assure them, the CIA, that repercussions would not occur from the ending the relationship?"

Again, the kitchen became silent.

Alexander continued. "There is a need for a mediator. It appears that slayers have somehow intervened in a historically functional relationship between vampires and the CIA and brought discord, and the discord is to their advantage. The CIA and vampires need to meet." He sat at the table with me and pulled a black address book from inside his suitcoat pocket.

"That is your father's personal telephone book. You will see names labeled with companies and titles. I am sure the information you need is in there ... and with your forgiveness, I must retire." He stood from the table, nodded his head at me, and left us in the kitchen. Without being fed my father's blood, he was weakening and becoming human again.

"He's right," Marcus said, coming to the table and sitting. "The slayers could be playing the vampires and the CIA."

Juanita pulled a chair from the table and sat. My mind went to Thomas and Detective Moss.

I had labeled Moss's file *Slayer Washout,* and his profile was on my screen. Marcus was looking at the file. "Suppose he didn't washout?"

"What?" I asked.

"Suppose he is functioning as he supposed to."

"Interesting," Juanita said, leaning towards the laptop.

I was still in the dark. "What are you saying?"

"Who has been present at each slayer attack?" Marcus asked.

I thought about the attack at my apartment, at Reginald's, and at the lake house. "Oh damn," I said. I got what he was saying. "You mean, he could be a slayer just playing a different part; not a washout, just a different type of slayer. You are saying Moss is a cop and a slayer."

"Exactly."

"Are we changing focus?" Natalie asked.

I looked to Juanita. She raised her brows, asking the same question.

Reginald said, "At present, all we have are guesses and speculations; that Chad guy could have been spinning a tale to save his life. We do not have facts. He told us a slayer paid the airport worker to put the bomb on Daniel's plane. That could have been a fabrication. What truth can we trust? Tell me, Ma, have you seen any sign of CIA involvement other than Chad saying so? I haven't. It was all police and slayers at my place." He looked at me, then Jocelyn.

Juanita lightly patted the table with an open palm. "We can be certain that the CIA has partnered with slayers. Why else would they want to meet?" she asked, looking directly at Reginald.

Marcus interjected, "We can be certain of that partnership for now, but that could change with mediation."

Jocelyn exhaled and sat on a stool. "God ... this is a mess."

"What about Thomas?" Juniata asked me.

I replied, "I think we should go get Moss. He could be leverage when we meet with the CIA and the slayers. And he can provide information."

"We are still meeting with them?" Natalie asked, sounding worried.

"Yes," Juanita and I agreed in unison.

"Yep, we should definitely meet. If we can avoid a war, we should, and we should a take representative from each clan in the city to the meeting," Reginald suggested.

"No, that is too many cooks in the kitchen. Later, when we have an idea of what the threat is, we can involve the other families," Juanita said, taking her eyes from Reginald to me.

"Yes, I agree. We need an understanding before we involve other families," I replied.

"But others are already involved – vampires across the country are discussing Daniel's death," Natalie insisted.

"I agree with your mom and Juanita, Natalie. We don't know enough to involve others," Marcus said.

"But they may be in danger, and meeting with the CIA could be a trap."

What Natalie was saying was true, and I understood her concern. But I said, "Later, Natalie. We will deal with the other families later."

She wasn't satisfied with what I said, but I think she understood.

"Ok, how do we get Moss?" Marcus asked.

I smiled at him and hunched my shoulders because I really didn't have a solid plan.

Jocelyn cleared her throat and offered, "From a military perspective, you have the element of surprise. He is not expecting to be kidnapped. The way I see it, Melody, you will walk into the trap with Reginald following you. You allow Moss and his partner to arrest you while Juanita enters through another entrance. Once the three of you are within the home, you overpower Moss and his partner. Marcus and I will be outside waiting for any CIA or the slayers to show themselves."

I was thinking the plan sounded good until Natalie said, "And if the CIA or slayers are present, you two will be able to hold them? I don't think so."

No one spoke. We all just looked at each other; then Jocelyn said, "Yeah, you should probably go with us." She smiled at Natalie, who did not return her smile.

Reginald huffed. "Yeah, it's sounding like we should all go."

In my head, I heard my daughter asking, "Why is she here? What? Reginald slept with her and now that makes her part of our group? She is not a minion or family. Why is she here?"

I answered, "She is a soldier for hire, and she is here due to my invitation, so be nice, Natalie Knight."

I turned my head to face my daughter and give her a smile. She looked away.

CHAPTER
- TEN -

"I hate you. You vampire bitch. Who the fuck told you to bite me? Who the fuck told you I wanted to live? Bitch, I had a shotgun in my mouth. I was trying to die. You stupid ass ho."

Reginald was the first vampire to be given the living-death in my home. He was the only man I had given the gift. He woke angry, and I didn't expect that. I tried to create the same waking environment Daniel had created for me; it worked with Natalie: a candle, a dark room, and a guiding, helpful voice. But Reginald woke wanting physical death. He jumped from the bed fuming with anger.

I spoke to him inside his head.

"Calm down."

His whole body twitched from hearing my voice inside

his head.

"Don't fucking do that. Get the fuck out my head," he yelled.

I remained in his head, "Calm down."

"Bitch, I said get out of my head."

He rushed me.

I told him, "Stop." He didn't stop, so I stopped him.

Ordering him to kneel, I dropped him to his knees. I stood from the table with the single burning candle and walked to him.

"You are mine, and you will respect me. Burn."

I set his mind on fire and his body felt it. He cried out in agony. "Cool off." He instantly became cool. "Freeze." His nude body trembled in chills on the floor. "Warmth," and the trembles stopped.

I circled him. Any confusion he had upon waking was gone. He knew who had the power.

"I can give you the physical death you claim to want. I can put you in that nothingness, or I can make you my slave and drag you through the living-death as my dog, or ... you can respect me and learn to be my son. Your old life, the one you didn't want ... is gone. You are no longer in Miami, and you are no longer Thaddeus Blakes. You are Reginald Knight, a vampire."

"Kill me, bitch."

"So be it." I drew my Falchion sword and was swinging the death blow when Natalie screamed in my head.

"No, Mother, wait! He doesn't know what he is saying." She walked into the room. "He's hurting from the life he had, and that pain is still holding him."

My blade was on the back of his neck.

"Let me try, Mother, let me talk to him."

My children only hear my voice in their heads; they don't hear each other. Reginald was surprised by my blade and to see someone else in the room. I kept the blade on the back of his neck; I was not convinced the living-death should be his until Natalie said "Please, Mother" out loud so Reginald could hear her. "He doesn't know how good this life can be; let me show him."

I answered, speaking so both of them could hear me, "He has six moons." I slid the sword along the back of his neck, slicing open his skin. "If he is not a vampire, he will be dust."

- Friday -

Thomas had done exceedingly well for himself. All we did – his mother and I – was pay for his education and buy him cars in undergrad and graduate schools. And for his graduation from journalism school, I did give him a nine-month world tour vacation, but his adult life accomplishments have all been his: the home in Beverly, the *Chicago Tribune* job, and the professional respect given to him by journalists all the across the country have all been gained through his hard work and determination.

"That's a really nice house" was Marcus's comment as we drove by checking the surroundings. We saw only the detective car and no sign of CIA vehicles or slayer vans. We were all in the limo except for Alexander. I couldn't wake him to drive us over. Minions sleep hard when they are weakened from lack of their maker's blood. Alexander had been Daniel's minion for over three hundred years; his existence would change with Daniel being gone.

Marcus had driven around three blocks and was parking

in front of the home next door to Thomas's. The car wasn't completely stopped when Juanita took her gaseous form and left the limo, leaving her clothes gathered at Natalie's feet. As I opened the door, Reginald transformed and circled my ankles. His clothes piled next to Jocelyn; she, Marcus, and Natalie remained in the limo watching me climb the stairs.

When I pressed the doorbell, the initial notes in Miles Davis's "So What" played. Thomas and his wife were serious Miles Davis fans. The porch was large enough to cast shadows that caused me to look over my shoulders several times.

The door opened, and I saw the almond-shaped and almond-colored eyes of my godson. He immediately embraced me and whispered "sorry" in my ear. His lean runner's body was in blue jeans and a white V-neck T-shirt.

"No, never," I told him. I stepped into the house and saw both Bowman and Moss standing in the foyer with guns drawn. I looked at the weapons, then back to Thomas.

"Your wife and the twins are upstairs, right? I truly hope these fine detectives would not have drawn their weapons in front of your family."

Neither holstered their weapon.

"His family is not your concern. We have a witness who saw you entering Castillo's hotel room approximately forty-five minutes before his time of death." Bowman, the white brunette with the bushy mustache, barked at me.

Moss said nothing; it was as if his hatred and contempt for me had gagged him. He jaws were tight, and his eyes seemed to be bulging with anger.

I looked back at Bowman and said, "Impossible, all that maid saw was the back of my yellow dress. No way she can identify me."

His eyes started blinking repeatedly, and he looked to the door behind me. My truthfulness shook him. I had no fear of the Chicago Police. His eyes returned to mine, and he continued the lie. "She identified your picture; turn around for the cuffs," he ordered, pulling handcuffs from under his suit coat.

"My picture, really?"

Maybe he didn't know I was a vampire. Maybe he was in the dark about what he was involved in.

Reginald's stream of gas was so thin he was almost translucent. Juanita didn't bother with hiding; she was thick as a storm cold. The hairs on the back of Moss's neck must have stood up because he turned his head as both were taking human form. I grabbed him by the back of his shirt collar and slung him into the foyer wall. I leapt into a flying roundhouse kick and struck Bowman across the chin with the blade side of my foot. He dropped to his knees and fell to his left, unconscious. Juanita and Reginald were picking Moss up from the ground. Thomas was rapidly backing from the action; he made it to the steps and ran up to his family. Reginald took the cuffs from Bowman's hand and cuffed Moss. We dragged both detectives into the dark early morning to a waiting Marcus and Jocelyn. Reginald shoved Moss to them.

Jocelyn ran up on the porch and pulled Thomas's front door closed and made sure it was locked.

"We better move their car. The police will track the vehicle," Marcus said, looking to Moss. "Where are the keys?"

I was not expecting it, but Juanita bared her canines and fed on Bowman. She went to the ground with his collapsing body. Marcus went through Moss's pockets and found the keys. Natalie pulled the limo up, and Marcus slung Moss into the closed backdoor, headfirst. Moss was stretched out unconscious in the grass.

"He talked too much," Marcus said. I took the cop car keys from him.

"Juanita and I will get rid of the car, and we will meet you at home tonight." I was speaking to all of them. "Juanita, bring the corpse." She was still feeding. Natalie brought me Juanita's clothes and phone.

They got into the limo and drove away as Juanita dragged Bowman's remains to the detective car. I got behind the wheel and she threw the corpse into the back seat. She sat down in the passenger seat, pulling the car door closed.

"I hadn't fed in eight moons. Didn't think I was in need until I smelled him."

Vampires feed when the need is present. I started the car.

"Junkyard?"

"Yeah, and I never thanked you for the idea; you know it has become very profitable. That was a good idea, Melody. Thank you."

I had considered buying the junkyard myself to export scrape metal to China because the market was expanding, and while discussing it with Daniel, he suggested I tell Juanita about it since the business required local hands-on management. I followed his suggestion, and she took to it like a fish to water. She ran the whole yard herself.

"Sunrise soon."

She didn't respond to my statement of the obvious. I guessed there wasn't much to say. We had less than forty minutes to drive out to Robbins, Illinois. She let out a lengthy breath, leaned the seat back, and closed her eyes.

We made it to the junkyard ten minutes before sunrise. She got out of the car and entered a code into the gate. It rolled open. I drove in, and she walked into the junkyard. A humungous Rottweiler, two high energy Pit Bulls, and a real wolf ran up to her with tails wagging. I don't like dogs, cats, or any animal pet. Juanita constantly reminded me that those canines had a job, and they were not pets, but she talked to them like children.

I pulled the car up to a ramp conveyer belt. When I got out, the dogs ignored me as always. I watched the gate closing and looked to the brightening sky. Juanita got into the driver's seat and drove the car up onto the ramp until the front wheels dropped into brackets. She got out of the car and walked to a big dangling black and gray switch box. I had seen the crusher squash and block cars before, but the process always amazed me. She pushed the red button, and I heard the water rushing and the gears and hydraulics kicking.

"Let's go in."

She walked to what looked like a tin shed and flipped up a panel and placed her hand against the screen. The door panels opened, and we stepped into her office/home. Juanita still lived at Daniel's, but she spent so much time at the junkyard that she added the comforts of home to her office: wall-mounted television, a king-sized bed, a walk-in jet shower, a sofa, a spin cycle, a treadmill, and a washer and a dryer. Her desk was in the center of it all with two large computer screens and an iPad.

I walked to the sofa and dropped to my butt.

"No CIA," I said.

Juanita answered with, "Or slayers."

"I was expecting to see both."

"So was I."

I pulled out the address book Alexander gave me and went to "P," looking for the name Pike.

"Look up Pike," Juanita directed.

"Yep, that's what I'm doing."

We both knew Pike worked with Daniel. I found the name and number and handed her the book. She pulled out her phone and dialed the number. She went to her desk and placed the phone in a cradle; it rang over a speaker system that was heard throughout the office.

"Pike" was heard through the speaker.

"This is Juanita Knight, Daniel Knight's daughter."

"You have my condolences. I see your clan hasn't wasted any time in seeking retribution. The bomber was found in a cell bone dry, and I am thinking Chad Oliver also fell to your clan."

Juanita didn't confirm his suspicions.

"I am calling in regard to tonight's meeting."

"Yes, with slayer representatives, myself, and three other division heads."

"I am confirming the meeting topic."

"It remains the same; vampires working with slayers within the CIA hierarchy."

"We have reason to believe that you are being deceived by slayers."

"Interesting. I am sure they are no more deceptive than vampires killing a police detective and smashing his remains within a block of steel or kidnapping another police detective."

His words told us they knew where we were and what we had done. There was no doubting that we were under surveillance.

"He is a slayer," Juanita answered.

"Yes, he may be, but presently he is a kidnapped police officer. Kidnapped by vampires who are speaking of other's deception. Vampires who act in their own interest while supposedly helping the CIA. We will see you at seven this evening."

The call ended.

"Damn," was all I could say. I reached out to Reginald and told him to "make sure Moss stays alive."

"Ok, Ma" was his answer.

Looking at her phone in the cradle, Juanita said, "They have a point. We do – we do what we want to do." Then a big grin crossed her face. "I guess we are not the best employees."

I wanted to grin with her, but anger for Pike's ungratefulness took hold on my attitude. Knowing the CIA could hear our conversation, I loudly stated, "But we still do the job. We offer them help; help that I am getting tired of giving. Daniel was the only reason I worked with them. Slayers killed Daniel, and now the CIA wants slayers to supervise us. Fuck the CIA, and fuck working with slayers. I'm not going to that meeting. Fuck them; this is some bullshit. I need to kill some more damn slayers – that will make me feel better." And I was dead serious.

Juanita grinned, understanding what I was doing. "Yeah, me too and maybe a CIA agent too. Fuck them." She screamed at the ceiling.

We had just resigned from the agency and threatened both the CIA and slayers. No more deceptive games were being played, at least not by us. Juanita's dogs started growling and barking, and they were instantly silenced. I heard what sounded like chains dragging. I got up from the sofa and followed Juanita to her bed. She pushed it aside and I saw the trapdoor. She opened it as we both heard the creaking. The shed, her office, began to sway forward. I went down the ladder to the sewer. Juanita was only halfway down because she was pulling the bed back in place. She closed the lid and slid the bolt latch over, locking the trapdoor.

Standing was temporary; we took four steps and had to begin crawling through the sludge. Juanita quickly transformed and I followed her lead. There were streams of daylight shining through, but we were successful at avoiding them. I didn't know exactly how far we had travelled, but the distance was substantial; she stopped and went up. We travelled through metal pipes, plastic pipes and aluminum vents, and air ducts. We passed through a vent and came out in an office. Juanita transformed back, and again I followed her lead.

It was a huge office. She picked up the phone and dialed Pike's number from memory. She put him on speaker, and when he answered, she said, "You know where I am, bitch." She sat at his desk and cut on his computer. She pushed the keyboard to me, and I quickly went to work.

"I don't have a clue as to what you think we know, what you are so afraid of the Knight clan exposing to the world, but rest assured, we will find out. I loved my dogs, and I considered them family."

Pike answered, "You know nothing that could hurt the agency. I and others just want you vile creatures removed from our ranks."

Juanita shook her head no, as if he could see her. "No, there is more to it. Your kind doesn't walk away from benefits, and we have benefitted the agency. You had to know slayers and vampires could never work together. So, there must be more to it."

Pike yelled, "You don't follow fucking orders." He hung up and the building started shutting down. I had been uploading most of his hard drive to my cloud while Juanita had him on the phone, and fortunately when the building's power cut off, the computer kept running long enough to finish the upload. His password was his office number backwards, his initials, and an exclamation mark. On his computer screen, he had a posted note that read "office number -!" – what an idiot. I got in on my third attempt.

CHAPTER
- ELEVEN -

"He is male, a natural aggressor. His transition will be different. You have only witnessed your own transformation and your daughter's, and your sisters raised you, so you really haven't seen human males transform. It will be a learning experience for you."

Daniel was smiling. I was not. He had come over because he sensed my frustration. We were sitting on my porch looking at the stars above the woods.

"And I think having Natalie helping is a good idea. Were you really about to decapitate him?"

"Yes. His words were vile, and his attitude was intolerable. Natalie saved him from eternal darkness. Her helping was her idea alone. I was finished with him."

"And what have you named him?"

"Asshole would be appropriate."

Daniel laughed out loud, rocking back in the rocker. He'd brought me two handcrafted rocking chairs for the porch.

"I think that would be a bit drastic. Driving across the lake, I thought of Reginald. Whether you see it or not, upon my demise, other families, other clans, will see him as the head of the Knight clan."

"Charlette is the oldest."

"She is female; her male hire would have been seen as the head, but she will not take a man or a woman – she will not pass on this gift. The angry boy you gave the gift to will be the head of this clan, so name him king; name him Reginald."

"It's funny. That is the name I gave him."

- Friday -

We emerged from the sewers at nightfall and swooshed to Daniel's home in anger. We moved through the night sky certain of our adversaries. Our enemies were the CIA and the slayers. We transformed to human form on Daniel's porch, and the first thing I noticed was that there were no lights on in the house or on the porch. Vampires don't need lights, but Jocelyn and Alexander should have been with them. My mind reached for my children, and I didn't get a response. I reached out again and again, but I didn't feel either of my children.

"Something is wrong," I told Juanita.

"Yes. I feel it." She pushed the door open and we walked in.

The first corpse we saw was Alexander's, lying across the top of the couch. He had been beheaded. Sitting on the floor against an armchair with an arrow in his chest and another in his neck was my son, Reginald, and he was a human corpse – which was impossible, but human blood was seeping from his wounds.

I dropped to my knees and crawled to my son. I placed my hand on his face. I had to touch him. I closed his eyelids.

Juanita was standing next to Alexander, looking into his wound; she said, "This is human blood, not minion."

I stood from Reginald and surveyed the room slower. Decapitated and leaning backwards against the bookcase was a still standing Marcus. His blood too was human red, not tinged with vampire green. My head was swirling because nothing I saw made any sense. I reached again for Natalie and still there was nothing.

Suddenly, stadium lights flooded the dark living room through windows and the front door. In the door entrance stood Moss and our sister, Charlette. The house lights came on, and from the kitchen entered Jocelyn and three slayers. My eyes returned to my sister Charlette; she was human. I smelled her. Moss was armed with what looked like a flame thrower. When I looked back to Joycelyn, she was armed with the same type of weapon.

Charlette spoke. "Sisters, don't fight. We have a way to remove the curse."

Both Jocelyn and Moss were taking aim with the strange weapon while Charlette spoke to us, and slayers were flooding the room. I wanted to hear what she had to say, but the weapons were fired. Juanita and I moved. A stream of red liquid barely missed us. As we were avoiding the red streams, three gaseous vampires swarmed the living room. They were buzzing through the room like angry hornets. I saw the liquid stream enter a cloud and one gaseous vampire instantly dropped to the floor and began transforming to human form; it was James Shore, one of Nelson Shore's brothers. Juanita and I were able to transform and follow the other two vampires from the house into the night.

We followed them to the lake and into a waiting seaplane. Inside the seaplane, we transformed back to solid form. We had followed Nelson Shore and his other brother Alvin.

Nelson Shore, with his dancer's build and pecan brown skin, spoke first as he sat between us on the bench seat. "We are flying to Racine, Wisconsin. A lot has changed, Melody Knight. A lot has changed in a day."

His darker brother, Alvin, was sitting in the pilot's seat, and he seemed to be having trouble transforming. He kept fading from gas to solid form. When he finally became solid, he was human. I smelled his fear. He started the seaplane while looking straight ahead. Every vampire in the plane had to smell him.

Nelson continued talking to us while looking at the back of his brother's bald head. "Earlier, I came to take Natalie to a concert. When I got here, they were being attacked. Charlette has betrayed us. We have Natalie, but I got there after the battle, after the slayers attacked with that weapon. I could not help the others."

There was nothing clandestine about the seaplane's takeoff. It was loud and attention gathering. We were airborne from the lake when stadium light beams from the ground passed over us. I had thought of buying a seaplane previously, and that night, flying above the lake with the Shores, I wanted to think about buying a seaplane, not my dead son, not Alexander, not Marcus, and not Charlette, my sister, betraying vampires, nor did I want to think about the once vampire that just turned human who was flying the plane. But ... it was Charlette and the human pilot that dominated my mind.

"The weapon?" Juanita asked.

Nelson released a lengthy exhale and put his gaze on Juanita.

"It changes a vampire; returns her to being human, and it takes a minion's power. From what I understand, Charlette came in with slayers, and she was instructing them on how to use the weapons."

I wanted to scream "liar" into his face, but I had seen Charlette standing next to Moss, and she was not fighting against him. Juanita and I looked at each other, seeing the other's pain and disbelief.

Juanita asked, "Human? Back to human?" Her eyes went to the pilot, Alvin Shore.

"Yeah, if a vampire is hit with the weapon as a gas cloud, his transformation is to human – not to vampire in human form, but an actual human. According to Natalie, when a vampire is in human form and hit with the weapon, there is a slight gaseous state, then they change back to human. She saw her brother go through it. And once we are human, the slayers have the advantage; the same is true when minions are stripped of their power; slayers have the advantage."

We were all looking at the back of Alvin's head.

"And Natalie?" I asked.

"I found her in the woods behind Daniel's house. They hit her fleeing in the gaseous state, but she made it to the woods. I found her crawling on her knees with slayers behind her. I attacked and killed them because they didn't have the weapon. Once I got her on the seaplane, she explained everything, and she told me you would be returning to the house. So, we came to get you."

"Thank you."

"No worries."

I wanted to ask was Natalie human or vampire, but he said she was hit by the weapon. Instead of asking, I watched his brother piloting the seaplane.

"Is Natalie ok?" Juanita asked.

I kept my eyes on Alvin.

"I don't know. She is waiting on you, Melody Knight."

CHAPTER
- TWELVE -

I had been living the living-death for over ten years when Daniel approached me about working with the CIA. He, Charlette, and Juanita had been involved with the agency since its founding. I asked Juanita if Daniel gave her a choice. She told me, "I didn't need a choice; it sounded like fun, so I did it."

I didn't say yes to his request right away because I knew the agency's history with African nations, Latin American nations, and Middle Eastern nations. I knew of the agency's involvement, their interference, and their dominance over smaller nations before I became a vampire. So, when Daniel asked me, I hesitated. We both knew he could command it and I would do it, but it wasn't a command; he gave me a choice. However, it was the actual assignment that convinced me.

Marcus and I were attempting to establish a Middle Eastern market share when Daniel had Chad Oliver reach out to me. He came to my home armed with a laptop and a folder of aerial photographs and graphs. The assignment he was proposing was related to the worldwide human organ market; his intelligence indicated that the market was being directed and controlled by the wrong companies, and if these "wrong companies" continued to control the market, the Western world could be held hostage in terms of heath care. He had five-year projections of the organ market expanding to a $51 billion industry.

The companies that were directing and controlling the markets were storing and shipping the organs in and from volatile areas. The two areas that Chad, his intelligence, and his superiors were concerned about were Iraq and Cairo. The governments of both nations had been uncooperative in motivating the companies to move. However, once the storage facilities had repeated problems, the CIA's plan was to offer safer facilities in Oregon and North Carolina. The repeated problems were my assignment.

I accepted the assignment because it sounded simple. I was thinking a couple fires and I would be on my way home; go in the facilities as gas, then transform back into human form and start the fires. Chad said, "No, fires are too easy to recover from, we need them hurting and looking for alternative storage facilities; talk to your sister, Charlette." *He closed the laptop and folder and left. I had Marcus drive me across the lake to Daniel's house.*

Charlette was sitting in the dining area studying at the handcrafted oak table we got Daniel for Father's Day. Charlette had returned to school to earn a PhD in biology.

"Dr. Knight," was my greeting to her.

She closed the book at looked at me sternly. "I thought you weren't going to work with the CIA; Chad just called me saying you would need my assistance?"

I sat at the table and sighed.

"I didn't say I wasn't going to work for them, and besides, Daniel wants me to."

She nodded her head yes. "Say no more. I understand. He really believes the agency brings justice and humanitarian equilibrium to the world. He thinks Americans are the good guys."

A door closed upstairs, and I heard Daniel saying, "I do not." He was speaking out loud and walking down the stairs. "I think they are the better guys. There are no good guys."

He joined us at the table and sat.

"America is a world power, financially and militarily. These powers allow them a guiding position; other nations follow their lead, and if we are at the table for their planning, if we are in the room, then we can have influence, and we gain knowledge by being present.

"True, Americans are not always the good guys, but they are the powerful guys, and we must be abreast of where the power is being applied; associating with the CIA gives us that knowledge."

His coal black eyes had settled on me, "And from what Marcus tells me, you are looking to expand into the Middle East freight trade, no? So, this is a win-win situation for you, Melody."

He was smiling, and I laughed because working with the CIA would help my business.

Charlette began, "It appears as though Chad wants an infection at both facilities, and he wants the media informed of the infectious outbreak. I have a bacterium in mind, one that the facilities must test for to be compliant with WHO policy.

"Once the bacterium is detected, the facility must close its doors, and the building can longer be used because the bacterium is reoccurring. If you can get plans of the facilities from Chad, I will show you where to place the samples, so they can be discovered during testing."

With Charlette's help, Marcus and I pulled off the first assignment without a glitch, and Marcus remained in Egypt establishing a business relationship that spanned throughout the Middle East to Turkey, Romania, and Ukraine. My working with the CIA became extremely profitable over the years, but all good things end.

- Friday -

There was a black SUV parked at the Shores' dock waiting for us. The windows were darkly tinted against sunlight, and we hurried from the seaplane to the vehicle. Nelson got behind the driver's seat. The last to board was Alvin. He seemed confused and overly concerned about his naked-ness. We had all transformed without any clothes, but Alvin was constantly covering his genitals with his pink hands.

Nelson was trying to console him by telling him, "It will work out, father will know something, relax. He will have a solution."

I doubted it. I had never heard of a vampire returning to human, so a cure couldn't possibly exist. I reached out again for Natalie, and again, nothing.

We, the Knights, had been to the Shores' home before.

Nelson's father, Justin, was as old as Daniel; they had lived through the transatlantic slavery, the American Revolution, and all the American wars as friends. They founded a railroad company together and still worked together in limited ways. Justin Shore only had three sons and no minions. He was an extremely private man.

Juanita and I were in the back seat of the black SUV. "How could she?" I asked her, referring to Charlette's betrayal.

"I told you, Melody, Charlette was tired of this life. She was tired of being a vampire. What was it she screamed – 'we have a way to remove the curse'? The curse, she called us cursed."

I heard the words Charlette screamed. "But maybe Daniel's death pushed her over some edge?"

But she was with them, and she was human.

"Maybe, but she is with the slayers now, and so is your soldier of fortune."

So much had changed so quickly. I watched Alvin Shore twitching with worry in his seat. A lot had changed for him too.

"Slayers or the CIA, I'm not sure which, but you are right; Jocelyn is the enemy."

The SUV pulled up to a metal barrier that looked like a solid wall. I didn't see an opening, but it opened a lot like Juanita's office door; two panels separated, and Nelson drove the SUV through. He pulled under a huge awning that blocked the early morning sun.

We were walking under the awning to the house when Nelson's bother stopped following him. He walked from us into the sunlight. We all stopped and stood still, watching him. He was standing in the early morning sunlight. He extended his arms high and spread them wide, and he looked directly up into the sun. When he lowered his head, he smiled at his brother and said, "It has been sixty years since I felt the sun. I forgot its warmth, its caress. And you know what, my knee hurts. It was a track injury." He walked from the sun, limping to us. He smelled happy, really happy.

* * *

Housekeeping obviously was not a priority for the Shores. Dust and fireplace ash were noticeable thick on almost every surface, and nits and flies flew through the house as if they were in a field. From the doorway, I saw the kitchen. There was a single bulb hanging from an orange cord. Under the lightbulb sat my daughter, and standing behind her was Justin Shore, Nelson and James's father. The leader of the Shore clan, and Daniel's friend. He was just as tall as Daniel but not as dark. Justin Shore's red hair and gray eyes gave his brown face a reddish tone.

Alvin hurried by us and walked into the kitchen first. Justin took several steps back away from his son. Alvin stopped his approach, turning away from his father. He walked past us and went up some stairs. We all entered the kitchen.

Natalie stood when she saw me and ran into my arms. I returned her hug. She was crying.

"The gift is gone. They took it from me."

She was shedding tears, but it wasn't despair, grief, or sadness emitting from her body.

Still in the embrace, holding me tight, she said, "Justin Shore said I cannot return to being a vampire. He said I am like a minion who returns to human form; I must remain human. The gift is only given once."

I returned the tightness of my daughter's embrace, then released her. I looked at Justin Shore. I knew minions couldn't return to being minions after they stopped drinking the blood of the vampire they served, but I never knew of a vampire returning to human. Who was Justin to say what could or could not happen? This was all new terrain as far as I knew.

"What are you basing that statement on?" Juanita asked Justin Shore before I could.

He leaned back against the sink and folded his arms across his chest. "During the second World War, vampires would help American troops during night battles; we had American uniforms that were passable on the battle fields, and we did help, but the problem occurred when vampires were seriously injured and not given time to heal on their own.

"When human medics saw the vampires' green blood, they treated it as an infection and gave vampires human blood plasma. The vampires were given intravenous blood transfusions, and depending on how much blood was lost, some returned to being human.

"Since the plasma was not digested but placed in the blood stream, it attacked the vampire cells, but it only happened to vampires who had lost severe amounts of blood and could not transform or heal themselves: those that stepped on mines, had limps chopped off, or suffered serious bayonet wounds in the abdomen. Any wound that caused major blood loss left a vampire susceptible to returning to human form after a plasma transfusion.

"Many vampires who were turned human begged me to bite them again. I did it twice, and each man died human;

the gift of the living-death did not return. There is no returning."

He looked from me to Juanita to Nelson, and finally to Natalie. "I wish it was different, but it isn't."

"I have to sit down." Natalie returned to sitting at the table. "I am so tired."

I recognized the emotion I smelled surrounding Natalie; it was acceptance. She had settled with her fate. "Maybe Charlette can help." I said my thought out loud.

"No," Natalie answered. "She is really with them, Mother. And so is Jocelyn. Charlette sprayed Marcus with the weapon and weakened him for the slayers. Jocelyn sprayed Alexander, but even as a human, Alexander killed a bunch of slayers. I believe it was Jocelyn who sprayed me once I transformed."

Juanita asked, "How did it feel getting hit by the weapon? The spray, what did it feel like?"

The four of us – Justin, Nelson, Juanita, and myself – were still standing and looking down on Natalie, who was sitting at the table. We vampires wanted to hear the answer.

"Heavy," she answered, "very, very heavy. I felt weighted. When the spray hit me, it was as if a force was dragging me to the ground, but I fought with everything I had to stay gaseous until I got out of that house; in the woods, the force overtook me, and I fell hard to the dirt. I couldn't stand and run, the weight was too much, so I crawled, trying to get away. All I saw was my hands moving in the dirt. It wasn't until Nelson picked me up that I realized I was safe.

"The weapon releases a red stream of steam. When it hits solid mass, it covers the body in a red cloud and for a quick second the vampire is gaseous – but instead of transforming into a cloud, they become human."

None of us spoke. Moments passed.

"We are lighter, less dense than humans," Juanita said. "What you said makes sense." She sat at the table with Natalie and so did I.

Nelson walked from the table to the stove and back to the table. "I never knew a vampire could return to being human."

Justin said, "I only saw it during the war."

This is war, I thought. We were fighting against the CIA and slayers.

"The slayers have a weapon powerful enough to eliminate the vampire species." I addressed Justin. I wanted to hear his opinion. "And they are working with the CIA."

His shoulders dropped and his head hung; he slightly raised his head and rolled his gray eyes up to me.

"You sound like your father, and you are making the same error we made hundreds of times before. There is no CIA, slayers, FBI, or military; it is only humans trying to kill vampires. Vampires have always thought if we worked with this group or that group things would be better, but in the end, humans fear vampires, and they should because they are our prey."

I thought of Charlette drinking from blood banks instead of feeding off of humans.

Alvin, the human son, walked into the kitchen and stood in the doorway. He was fully dressed with a pack on his back. I still smelled his happiness.

"I am taking the Porsche, and I transferred $5,000,000 to my personal account. I am keeping the Shore name; it's easier that way. I'm not sure how to handle the corporate concerns. I'm going back to Florida. I will call you both once

I get set up." He was speaking to his father and his brother, but only his brother answered.

"Are you sure?" Nelson asked him.

"Yes, I want to be human again."

His father, Justin, turned gaseous and left the kitchen.

Nelson extended his hand to his brother and said, "Talk to you soon."

And the once vampire left the kitchen without another word. Juanita looked at Natalie curiously.

Natalie laughed out loud. "I'm not going anywhere. We have accounts to balance."

Her words warmed my heart. I turned my head to Nelson and said, "I need a computer."

He nodded his head yes and left the kitchen.

Natalie's eyes were on mine. "I can live like this, Mother. I can live as a human. When you gave me the gift, I didn't have a life. I had murdered a man and was ready to go to hell. That is not my state of mind now. I have a life and many reasons to live."

She reached to me and covered my hands with hers. I felt the weight she spoke of; her hands were heavy atop mine.

CHAPTER
- THIRTEEN -

When I was walking back home from Jackson, Mississippi, to Chicago, my view of humanity changed slightly for the better. I met people who didn't know me from Adam; people who pulled along dark roadsides to offer me help because they saw me walking. People drove me miles out of their ways because they didn't want to see a woman walking at night.

I was fearless on my walk, and most humans didn't understand the courage. They thought I was crazy choosing to travel at night instead of during the day. I walked so I could experience the countryside. I seldom transformed. I bathed in lakes, streams, and rivers. I followed deers and bears. I climbed trees, and I spent more days than I expected resting in their hollows avoiding sunlight. I often ran alongside the interstate traffic at night, pacing trucks running at a hundred plus miles an hour; that's what I was doing, pacing a truck when I met another night traveler, Tina Adomako.

I had blazed by her under a viaduct. I sensed her despair, and it slowed me down. I stopped about a quarter mile past her. I walked back to her not to feed, but to help. She had waddled past the viaduct. She was a large woman with very short legs. When I approached her on the side of Interstate 65, she said, "Not since home have I seen someone run that fast, and you are the fastest runner I have ever seen. I barely saw your legs moving. You are very fast."

Her words sounded lighthearted, but a heavy sadness weighted the air around her despite her tone. I extended my hand to the roly-poly woman, and we shook hands. She was literally a beachball with legs.

"I am Melody Knight."

"Aw, I am Tina Adomako."

We were yelling because trucks were continuing to speed past.

"Why are you walking on the interstate, Tina?"

She stood still, looking into traffic and not at me. "I read in the newspaper yesterday that a truck struck and killed a young mother, and the owners of the trucking company paid her family almost three million dollars."

The road dust and the small pieces of debris that were left in the wake of the speeding trucks was assaulting our skin, but Tina didn't flinch or blink from the assault. She was watching the trucks, and then I understood; she was planning on getting hit by a truck.

"That had to be a very painful death for the young mother."

"Perhaps, but the end should come quickly."

"Do you have a family?"

"I have a son." She looked from the traffic to me. "He is in the hospital."

We two women were standing face to face on the side of the interstate smelling truck exhaust. I asked her, "And you are thinking his life will be better without you?"

She slowly nodded her head yes.

"Yes, that is so."

I told her what I knew.

"Most trucking companies cannot afford to pay out a million dollars. Most of these trucks are driven by independent owners, and their insurance policies will only pay out fifty thousand dollars for accidental death. The chance of a corporately owned truck running you over is very slim."

Her eyes were still watching oncoming traffic.

"You sound very informed."

"I work in logistics."

"I will pick a well-lit truck. The ones with company names on the side are owned by corporations, correct?"

"That is no guarantee; an independent driver might be hauling a corporate trailer. There are too many variables involved in selecting a corporate-owned truck."

Her eyes widened and she crouched down, preparing to leap. I was not going to let her kill herself.

I wrapped my arms around her head and chest and jumped with her over the interstate railing. We were airborne for about fifty yards. I brought us down gently into some marshy farmland. I rolled free of her and stood. She remained in the marshy soil on her knees.

She screamed, "You won't be here tomorrow; I will do it then. Even fifty thousand dollars is better for him than me."

She was serious. I was certain she would make another attempt when I left. So, I kicked her in the head, knocking her out. I reached out to Daniel.

"I have a woman that I need to impress. Can you send Alexander with the chopper and my laptop?"

"He is on his way."

While Tina was unconscious, I drained half her blood. Alexander helped me load her into the chopper. There was only one hotel in Lexington, Kentucky, that had a landing area for chopper. I rented the presidential suite and Alexander helped me carry her in.

Once we got in the suite, he told me, "She looks Ghanaian, like my people. What is her name?"

"Tina Adomako."

A huge smile crossed his face as he placed her on the couch.

"I know many with the last name Adomako from Kumasi. Yes, she is Ghanaian."

He looked at her fondly and left.

Tina opened her eyes, rubbing the temple I kicked her in.

I quickly told her, "My apologizes for the kick, but I had to pause your thinking." Her gaze was curious, but she didn't ask a question.

"Come here, sit at the desk with me."

She was weak from the blood I took, but she walked to the chair and sat. To her left was a chair with new clothes, and before her was a crystal gauntlet filled halfway with my green blood. I was sitting at the suite's desk; she was in the chair next to me. I had my laptop open to my business page.

Her hand went from her temple to the marks on her neck that my bite left.

"I was in a helicopter?"

"Yes, you were."

"And you jumped with me in your arms from the highway far into a field?"

"Yes, I did."

"And you were running as fast as the trucks."

"That is also true."

"And there was a Ghanaian man here?"

"Yes, you may see him again."

She glanced around the room and said, "I have cleaned this room, many times; I worked as a maid at this hotel."

I wanted to tell her, no more. But I wasn't sure how she would respond to my offer. Her possibly being Ghanaian made her more appealing for what I was considering.

"Look here and tell me what you see." I wanted to see if she could grasp the service I provided from the webpage.

She reviewed the page then adjusted the laptop so she could see it better. She placed her finger on the mouse pad and navigated through the website.

"This company takes products from one country to another by airplanes, ships, and trains. And they are vague about their fees for the service."

"Yes." I smiled at her. I had to be vague because each situation was different. Set prices would have driven me to bankruptcy. "This is my business. I help people move freight, and the man that was here does this for me in Ghana, but he is my father's minion, and he has other responsibilities. However, he is willing to train his replacement."

"Minion?"

"Yes. He is a blood servant who has worked for my father for over two hundred and fifty years."

"Aw," she dismissed my words with a flick of her hand and looked from the laptop to me. "You are speaking *foolishness."*

I turned the laptop back to me. "No, I am not."

She considered my words, and asked, "Is your father a priest?"

"No."

"A witch then?"

"No, he is a vampire."

"Aw. Oh, I see. Then he is a priest. Only priests can drink the blood of life."

I did not argue with her because of the certainty in her voice; instead, I asked, "What will stop you from killing yourself and leaving your son motherless?"

She sat erect in the chair; "Nothing" was her answer. "His life is worse with me as his mother."

"Why?"

"Because I have nothing to give him. I cannot even buy his asthma medicine." She stood from the chair but sat right back down. "He was born here in America. If I die, he becomes a ward of the state, and the country will take care of him. America will become his parent. With me, he will starve or die from his sickness."

I pulled her attention back to my screen. "Look here," I opened my inquiries. "These are my potential customers: three Ghanaian companies looking to ship to America and Canada and one Cuban company looking to ship to Ghana."

"This website is really your company?"

"Yes. And these inquiries could easily generate over $250,000."

"That is a small fortune."

"It is, but the handling of the job takes a minion, one with abilities beyond a human."

"Why?"

"It requires international travel, a mastery of most languages, and the ability to process information at computer speed."

"And the Ghanaian man that was here can do those things?"

"Yes, quite easily, but he is my father's minion, not mine."

"But your father is a vampire priest, so he has many minions. Ask him for one?"

"No, any minion he creates is his blood-bound servant."

"Aw, I understand."

"Alexander, the Ghanaian man that was here, is a millionaire several times over."

"No?"

"Yes, and he can stop being a minion whenever he chooses. He can return to being human when he chooses. He is not a vampire. The only blood he drinks is my father's, which gives him minion abilities."

"Aw, he drinks the priest's blood and gets some of the priest's powers. And he can return to being a man?"

"Yes."

"Whenever he wants?"

"Yes."

"And you say he has been serving your father for two hundred and fifty years?"

"Yes."

"And he is very rich with superpowers?"

"Yes."

"And this green drink before me, this is some of your father's blood?"

"No, that is my blood."

"Your blood? Aw, that is why you can run with trucks.

You are a minion too?"

"No, I am a vampire in need of a minion."

"Aw. Oh, so this is your blood?"

"Yes."

I stood and transformed in front of her. I moved through the suite at near light speed. I returned to human form and dressed.

Her eyes were wide in amazement. She picked up the gauntlet and asked, "And I will become rich?"

"Yes, beyond what you can imagine."

- Saturday -

Nelson had brought us a laptop, and he was sitting at the table with Juanita, Natalie, and me. Once I accessed my cloud account, opening the CIA upload gave me reason to exhale, as we were about to get on the offensive in a big way. I didn't download the file onto Nelson's computer; I was hoping the cloud security would offer us some cover for a while.

"Is this what it looks like?" Nelson asked.

"If it looks like a CIA file, then yep. It is what it looks like," Juanita said, scooting her chair closer to the laptop screen.

"This should give us an advantage because everyone knows the CIA is always up to some mess." Natalie also scooted her chair closer to the laptop.

The first file I opened was titled Fernando Castillo. He was the man I'd fed on in the hotel; the one Chad had assigned me to observe only. Pike had Castillo's accounting records dating back fourteen years.

"Wow, look at that." Juanita pointed to a line of business labeled Legacy Airlines. Her finger traced numbers that merged into a column labeled Rollins Transportation. "That only makes sense if they are one and the same." Her finger remained on the screen. "Rollins Transportation is one of Daniel's Companies."

Rollins Transportation had its own file, which I opened. There were only three names under the file: my father's, Alvin Shore, and Justin Shore.

There was another file labeled media. Inside the file were video clips labeled EXPOSURE. We watched the video news clips and saw tragedy after tragedy involving Castillo's Legacy Airlines and Legacy Transportation; there was no mention of Rollins Transportation until one of the last clips.

There was a Cuban reporter on the screen, and he was linking Rollins Transportation to the Legacy Corporations and Castillo. He painted Rollins Transportation as the fall guys for any Legacy Transportation mishap or accident.

He reported that when Legacy Airlines was sued for a plane that crashed into and destroyed five farms, the crash was ruled pilot error, and the pilot turned out to be a Rollins Transportation employee, and Rollins Transportation paid all the damages.

The very next video clip was recorded with no sound; it was of the reporter's funeral. The next file I opened was labeled AGENCIES. It appeared as though Rollins Transportation corporation owned eight adoption agencies across the globe.

Nelson stood up from the table. "Rollins Transportation is my father's company; he and Daniel have owned it for over a hundred years."

"That doesn't mean it wasn't a CIA company; Daniel

consulted with the agency." Juanita said.

The next file I opened contained newspaper articles on missing children. All the children went missing on the same date. Each agency was missing two children, and in each city the media responded to the missing orphans. But the article that shook me to bone was reported by my godson in the *Chicago Tribune*. The article was titled, "Sixteen Children Die in a Legacy Transportation Freight Car."

"Were those the missing children?" Juanita asked me.

"Why would they be in the same file if they weren't?" Natalie was still reading the article.

"Why would they take them to be killed in a freight car?" Nelson asked.

"Something went wrong; this is only the tip." Juanita said.

"You are right; there must be more." Natalie said.

"A lot more," I said.

I was going to say more, but the entire back wall of the kitchen exploded, and sunlight flooded the room, and an equally powerful explosion happened at the front of the room. The was no ceiling, and there was no escaping the sun. I was on fire.

CHAPTER
- FOURTEEN -

It was amazing how quickly I accepted Daniel's family as my own. Charlette and Juanita became my older sisters. I was the baby, and Charlette was the oldest, and we each took to those roles. Each of my sisters felt it was their duty to advise and direct my actions, and most times I listened. If I had questions, I would ask them before Daniel, and if they couldn't answer, I would ask Daniel. But there was one question that stumped the whole family, and it was never answered to my satisfaction.

I started with Juanita; Daniel had arranged a flight to New York for Juanita's birthday. She and I were the only passengers on the small jet. The pilot and the attendant were vampires. There were only eight passenger seats on the jet; we had been the only passengers to New York, and we were *the only passengers on the return trip.*

Daniel had secured us third row seats for "The Lord of the Rings Musical." Juanita was all grins throughout the entire play. I watched her eyes actually sparkle. She was a big fan of fantasy books and movies; going to the play was the perfect gift for her. It was the play that sparked my question. Our jet seats were fully reclined and there was no turbulence as we smoothly flew towards Chicago.

I asked her, "Where did Gollum come from?"

She turned her head to me. "Have you seen The Hobbit movies?" She asked as if all sane people in the world had seen the movies and knew where Gollum came from.

"No" was my answer, and I started to say I wasn't a nerd, but I kept that comment to myself.

"Gollum was a Stoor Hobbit from the river people. Watch the first movie, and it will answer most of your questions."

That wasn't going to happen, I told her, because "I don't have any more Lord of the Rings or Hobbit questions. Gollum just seemed such an odd character, and I wondered about his origin, much like I wonder about ours."

She brought her chair up from the reclined position, and in true Juanita fashion she became defensive. "What? Ours who? The Knights or all vampires? And are you comparing us Knights or vampires to Gollum?"

I brought my chair forward as well. I had learned to meet Juanita head-on in debates or any kind of challenge or else she would just walk all over me.

"I think any obsessed creature, man, vampire, or dog can be Gollum. If one covets any item over interpersonal relationships, abnormalities arise from the coveting."

Juanita's smile returned to her face, and she began

nodding her head in the affirmative.

"Yes, yeah, I can see that. Obsession perverts any thinking creature's behavior. I guess anyone can become Gollum."

Since I had her attention, I returned to my original question. "Gollum got me thinking about origins, and I was wondering where vampires came from?"

Her shiny jet-black eyebrows went up. "What?"

"I mean, Dracula is fiction. Where did real vampires come from? Obviously, we are not devil demons; so, where did we come from?"

She looked at me, and I saw the decision making occurring on her face. She answered with, "I thought about it before, maybe around the second year of living as a vampire. Everything I researched said we were fictional characters, and in fiction we have several beginnings. But I put all the fiction aside – I had to because it all pointed to Europe, and in reality, I could find no vampire whose family lineage reached beyond America, none."

I sat up further in the seat. "Wait, are you saying vampires started in America?"

She relaxed in the seat and turned her body to face me. "What I am saying is I talked to six vampire families, and of the six none can trace their beginnings past colonial America. That is what I am saying. Perhaps someone with a wider network of associates may fare better in the research."

The pilot's cabin door opened, and I saw the attendant flying the plane. I looked to Juanita, and she had seen the same thing. We both were about to object, but the short, round-faced, pudgy pilot stepped from the cabin to us, and he left the cabin door open. We could all see the attendant pilot.

His ears and forehead were tanned darker than the rest of his pink face. He was smiling, showing bright teeth. He walked to our seats.

"I was not eavesdropping, but all conversations are overheard on such a small craft. Do you mind if I add my two cents?"

I didn't and looked to Juanita, who hand gestured for him to continue.

"I have lived the living-death for four hundred and fifteen years. I was given the gift at twenty-seven. My family were French furriers, and I had to come to the New World because the trappers that worked for us kept quitting. We extended money for explorations only to be left financially drained. Trappers would arrive and once on the shores of the New World, they would abandon our previous contracts and work to build their own wealth, so I came to the New World myself to hunt and trap as I had done in France and Italy.

"Under my supervision, our profits surfaced and increased rapidly. I didn't limit us to only fox hides. We did racoon, wolf, buffalo, rabbit, and coyote. I had a five-man party up in northern Wyoming. I had sent two north, one west, one east, and one south. I built a good fire and began preparing pelts for the ride west when this Crow woman transformed from cloud to naked woman. I pulled the knife from the pelt and stood up.

"I was scared, but she was naked, and I'd not seen a naked woman in over a year." He was smiling and laughing at the memory. "Later, she told me I was the easiest man she ever given the gift to. I didn't put up much of a fight. I had never heard of a vampire before becoming one. I tried to live as human for months after she bit me, but it was pointless. Night Bird Feather, the woman that gave me the gift, kept communicating with me in my mind. I might have been the easiest to take, but I was the most stubborn when it came to joining her family."

He stopped talking and ran his fingers through his thick, curly black hair. He continued with, "We had sex before she bit me, and we kept having sex after she gave me the gift. I didn't want to be her son, which was how the other three vampires in her family wanted to see me. Our relationship was a problem for them at first, but eventually ... me always being at her side, me running our fur-trading business, and me taking her to France allowed them to see that I wasn't a son, and I wasn't going anywhere.

"It took over a hundred years to meet another European vampire; she was an indentured servant from Ireland that had run away from a Mississippi plantation, and she was bitten by an African runaway slave who was father to a community of vampires living on an island in the Carolinas. As time passed, and the longer the Europeans stayed, more became vampires; but like you said, I have never met a vampire that wasn't given the gift here. And I know at least thirty families, and all their heads were gifted here."

He still hadn't answered my question, but Juanita had been listening to him very closely. "So, you think vampires started here, in America?" she asked him.

"What I'm saying is I never met one who wasn't from here. That's all I'm saying."

"Where did vampires start?" I asked him.

"I don't know, my best guess is here. We know as much about our origin as humanity does about theirs; humans say they began in Africa, or Asia, or Ukraine, or Mexico, and some even say aliens from outer space. I stopped trying to figure out vampire origin after two hundred years of *vampire life."*

He put his hand on the small of his back and leaned back to stretch his back muscles.

"Aliens? I never heard that before, but I like that option, and it makes sense to me." Juanita smiled – no, she grinned at me. "I am going with aliens."

- Sunday -

I woke with my hands and feet in leather restraints, and when I say woke, I am referring to waking from sleep – which was something that hadn't happened in thirty-seven years.

I was restrained in a hospital bed and snatching at the restraints when the memory came clear my mind. They had blown up the house, and I was on fire. All my strength left me with that realization. I stopped pulling at the restraints.

My head was facing the window, and I saw the sunlight shining through the vertical blinds. It took me seconds to recognize that I was lying in the sunlight.

"I tried to give life back to Juanita."

The spoken words startled me. I thought I was alone, but I recognized the voice. It was Charlette. She was sitting under the wall-mounted television.

"She was ablaze and still avoided the stream. I wanted to save her."

I wanted to scream "lying bitch" in her face. Instead I said,

"Save her? You are working with the enemy – with slayers and the CIA."

She stood and left the room.

"Bitch," I said quietly, only because I didn't have the energy to yell it. I was physically drained.

Natalie and Nelson came through the door, and the smile that crossed my face gave me the energy to try and sit up, but the restraints held me. They came to the bed, and Natalie bent down and embraced me.

"Mother, I thought you were dead until Charlette came and got me out of that cell."

She held my face and kissed me, and another longtime-gone thing happened; I cried. Tears ran down my face. I hadn't cried since my wedding day. It was so good to see Natalie, and we stayed cheek-to-cheek for moments.

Into my ear, she said, "She told me so much."

"Who, baby?"

She stood up.

"Charlette, Mother. She explained a lot, but there is a lot she does not know. I think we should work together. She's not the trader we thought. She gave me this laptop, so we could explain things to her."

I looked to Nelson, and he was human as well. I asked him, "Your father?"

His lowered his head. "I don't know. The slayer attack was so quick. I don't know where he is."

Charlette returned to the room with a nurse who came to the bed and released my restraints.

"We were afraid of you injuring yourself. Some who are converted back attempt to kill themselves, but I should have known that wouldn't be the case with you, Melody."

"Anything else, Dr. Knight?" The nurse asked Charlette.

"No, that will be all, thank you. Oh, don't forget what I requested earlier."

"I won't, doctor."

The nurse left and Charlette walked back to the chair under the television and sat. Natalie and Nelson took the chairs in front of the window. I threw the sheet back and sat up in the bed. Someone had dressed me in a white track suit with white sweat socks.

"It was CIA funds that allowed me to complete my research. The conversion mist was completed and became functional five days ago. I tried it on myself before I used on anyone else. Pike was there in the lab. There were no slayers. I didn't develop the mist to be a weapon used against vampires. That was not my intent."

Unlike Natalie, I didn't want to understand Charlette. She betrayed us. "Well, that's what the fuck happened." I knifed my words at her, but she didn't blink.

"Pike involved the slayers without my knowledge. He gave them the mist without telling me. But there is more, and when the time is right, I will share it all with you."

She didn't sound like she was lying. She was my sister; I knew her tones, and she sounded truthful.

"You were there; you were at our house and the Shores' giving directions to the slayers," Natalie accused.

"Yes, I was, because without my supervision the mist was killing vampires, not converting them back to human. The slayers destroyed twenty vampires before Pike asked for my assistance and informed me that they were trying to use the mist. It was either help the slayers or witness the annihilation of vampires.

"I developed the mist for myself and others that wanted a cure. For others that were tired of the living-death and wanted to return to life. For those who wanted to reverse the curse."

I decided right then, with those words, that the woman

sitting under that television was no longer my sister.

"Curse? What are you talking about? What happened to you, Charlette? You accomplished so much with the living-death. How were you cursed?"

She leaned back in the chair and crossed her legs at the knees. The red bottoms of shoes her didn't match her doctor's coat. She had a charcoal black pantsuit with gray pinstripes on under her doctor's coat.

"Taking the life of others to live is a curse. Drinking human blood to live is a cursed existence. Living for two hundred years is a curse. All of my human family is dead. Do you know how long I have lived as a vampire? Two hundred and twenty years. I was twenty years old when Daniel gave me the gift. I am twenty again, but twenty with over two centuries of experience. So yes, I was cursed."

I rose from sitting on the bed and walked to the window. I was standing in the sun facing her.

"Juanita, your sister, was killed with your weapon. Fuck your intentions. Slayers and the CIA are using your weapon to kill vampires. And because of your mist, I have been weakened in the fight. Like Juanita, I did not want to be human. I was not cursed. Daniel gave me a gift. He gave me the living-death when I wanted everything to end.

"And what gave you the right to take the gift he gave me? Nothing. Nothing gave you that right. You have taken power from me, you have taken time from me, you have taken my father's gift from me. And why? Because you thought it was best?"

She didn't look away, and all three of us were staring daggers at her.

"None of you have lived more than fifty years as a vampire. I know what is ahead for you. I did what was best."

If I could have swooshed across the room and slapped her silly, I would have, but my swooshing was gone.

Natalie blew a long breath. "There is a lot she doesn't know, Mother. And after going through the files in more detail, I found it worse than what we thought." She pulled the laptop from her under arm. "If you don't mind, Charlette, we'd like to share some information with you."

Natalie stood from the chair and walked to the bed, and we all, including Charlette, followed her. She placed the laptop on the bed and opened a file.

CHAPTER
- FIFTEEN -

When I asked Charlette "What do you believe concerning the origins of vampires?" she stopped painting.

She was recreating the image of a mouse that had been caught in a trap and killed. She had set up her easel and brushes right where the death happened, next to one of the unlit dining room laps. The mouse obviously had been running along the baseboard when the trap sprang and took its life.

Charlette had touched nothing, the room was just as dark as it was when the mouse was killed, and her painting captured the darkness. I remember thinking that only vampires would be able to see the details.

Charlette answered my question with a query of her own.

"Why do you ask?"

Her brush was still in her hand, but she wasn't adding to the canvas.

"Because I've heard aliens, which I am not ruling out, and the fictional origins are all European, which doesn't really speak to the vampire families that have roots here in America, and the fiction takes the demon aspect, which I totally cannot accept."

The brush dangled down loosely between her thumb and forefinger.

"No, I mean why do you care? You have a great existence; accept it for what it is. You were given a gift; enjoy it."

She squatted and examined the mouse closer.

"I'm not looking a gift horse in the mouth, Charlette. I see all the benefits of the living-death. I don't think wanting to know where vampires began is ungrateful. I am merely curious."

Charlette stood. "I understand curiosity completely. I wanted to know our origin so badly that I questioned every vampire I knew and saw. Some made up origin histories just to get rid of me, and I am including Daniel in the group. I was purposely giving you a hard time because we all ask the question or at least wonder about it." She placed the brush on her palette.

"I have heard alien theory before, but that doesn't sit well with me because I want to know what else the aliens did. What, the aliens just dropped vampires off and left without any record of being here, no note or directions for vampires on how to contact them, nothing? That theory, that guess, about aliens is wanting at best. Daniel's reasoning was better."

She began mixing white paint with blue, making a light gray appear on the tip of the brush. "Daniel believes vampires are a genetic mutation; he theorizes that a human gene changed after smallpox ravished the First Peoples and after the buffalo decimation caused famine throughout the land. He believes vampires developed as a survival mutation. But his idea is just as flawed as aliens; his theory demands that baby vampires grow up and procreate. Vampires are not born; we are not living beings, so we are not mutations."

She had a point – we were not alive, and vampires don't grow up from childhood

"What are we?" I asked.

"We were human, so our origins are human. Every vampire was a human."

I considered what she said. Vampires could not have a separate origin because we came from humans.

"So, you are saying our origin is human?"

"Of course."

She mixed the light gray on the brush tip with the black on the palette.

"I think there was a sickness, a plague, and cannibalism allowed some to survive. The cannibalism morphed into drinking blood, and I think the cannibals were so few in number that they hid from the non-cannibals. Biological changes must have occurred and cannibals that were human somehow became vampires feeding off of humans. Those who were fed on that did not die also became infected, increasing vampire numbers. And there you have it, my guess." She had a smirk on her face, but I could tell she was serious. Her guess made sense.

Her attention went back to her painting. I stood there in the darkness considering all she said, and then I thought *about how I became a vampire. I thought about Daniel transforming from gas to man right in front of me; that was not of earth. Her guess was logical; however, I agreed more with the alien theory.*

- Sunday -

Natalie was trying to bring Charlette up to speed; we were all standing at the hospital bed listening intently.

"This is the file we were reviewing when your people attacked us. It clearly shows that Pike was aware of those children on the freight car before they died.

"See here, there were three previous times when children were shipped this way, and each time Rollins Transportation paid Legacy Transportation for moving the children."

Much to my agitation, Charlette was not recognizing the depth of the information. Everyone else was looking at the laptop, and the facts were clear. She leaned closer to the screen. "Could you scroll back?"

I exhaled loudly, but Natalie did scroll back.

"You see here, it doesn't say children; it reads freight."

Natalie replied, "Yes, but these freight shipments correspond with missing children reports from the orphanages; the freight shipments have the same dates and origin location as the missing children reports."

Charlette flipped her eyes up from the screen to Natalie. "Oh ... I see." Her tone was filled with so much caring that I had to look at her. She returned to reading. "How many children were forced to travel this way, and what was the destination?"

Natalie answered, "Hundreds; groups were taken to Egypt and Iran. At least four groups a year from each agency."

One of those groups of children was why I killed Fernando Castillo, and hearing the names of the countries gave me pause.

"To where?" Hearing Egypt and Iran sparked a thought – no, an actual memory of my first agency assignment.

"To two medical facilities, one in each country," Natalie answered.

I asked, "Not Jenkins Holdings and Pristine Medical?" The names moved from my mind as if the assignment was the day before.

"Yes, you named them both." Natalie looked up from the laptop to me. "How did you know that?"

I couldn't answer her because something physical was going on with my body. My head was beginning to pound, and I took a couple of wobbly steps. I had to grab ahold of the hospital bed mattress to steady myself.

"Are you ok, Mother?"

I didn't respond because the pounding was serious. "Mother?" Natalie stepped closer to me.

"I'm ok." I answered, but I wasn't. My back was starting to tighten and spasm. I forced out an answer. "Those were the two companies from my first CIA assignment. We caused the companies to relocate by infecting them with a biological agent; I thought they had closed down."

Natalie shook her head to the negative. "No, Mother. They are open and receiving regular monthly payments from Rollins Transportation."

Charlette took a step back from the bed and laptop.

"I remember that. The companies were housing human

organs." Her index finger went to her forehead, and it was rubbing her temple, a gesture I'd seen her do hundreds of times when she was thinking deeply.

My unsteadiness increased. I needed to sit down in a chair or lie down in the bed.

"Wait, and these children from the orphanages were taken there, to a place that housed human organs?" Nelson asked, looking at me as if I had answers.

My back and legs cramped so viciously that I exhaled in pain. Charlette came to me and gently took my arm and guided me to one of the chairs by the window. I was in too much pain not to accept her help.

Quietly, she said, "I'm not sure why, but it appears some vampires experience sever muscles spasms after the transformation. A nurse will be bringing you something that will help." She was looking me in the eyes as if her words meant more than what was heard.

Once I was sitting, Charlette returned to the laptop. "Tell me everything you think you know," she requested from Natalie. I wanted to stand and tell her not to talk to my daughter in that arrogant tone, but back spasms held my lips tight and my body in the chair.

I was gripping the arms of the chair so tight I was afraid my fingernails would tear into the beige vinyl. When I looked down at my hands, I saw them go gaseous then return to solid. It happened three times within seconds. I said nothing and placed my hands under my thighs.

"Mother and Juanita uploaded these files from Pike's office computer, and the ones we've opened seem to link the CIA to Rollins Transportation and Legacy Airlines. There appears to be eight orphanages located across the world where children are being taken. They are delivered by

Legacy or Rollins Transportation to either Jenkins Holdings in Egypt or Pristine Medical in Iran. That is what the files are telling us, so far."

No one spoke as Charlette glanced from person to person. "What you are implying is inconceivable." Her glance settled on me.

Natalie took a step back from the bed, and then she turned and faced the window; she didn't look at Charlette or the laptop. If my daughter had still been a vampire, she would have turned gaseous and left the room; she hated being around people who could not make logical correlations.

"I'm not making an implication; we are simply following a trail. However, the indicated end of the trail is dreadful." Natalie walked to the window, standing in the sun with her back to the bed and laptop.

Only Nelson was still looking at the laptop. "Wait, are you all saying the CIA is using kids, orphans, for their organs?"

No one answered him. I heard him, but I was worried about my alternating hands being discovered. They felt solid, so I eased one from my thigh, and it was flesh.

"The CIA heads cannot be aware of this." Charlette sounded hopeful.

"Pike is aware," I answered.

"That's for sure." Natalie walked back to the laptop.

"And now we are aware," Nelson stated.

While looking at Charlette's back, anger gathered inside my head. I asked her, "Were you human when you killed the man that placed the bomb in Daniel's plane?"

Charlette sucked her teeth – another gesture of hers that I knew intimately; it meant my question irritated her.

"I was." She turned to face me. "Daniel was my father, and I swore to avenge his death, but Pike and the CIA needed Daniel. The CIA would not have been party to his death, and this thing with the children ... I don't believe we have enough information to form a conclusion."

Her denial of the obvious made my eyes blink involuntarily. My body seemed to be doing a lot of involuntary movements since my return to humanity.

"Did Daniel know about the mist you were working on?"

"No."

"You do know the CIA wants vampires removed from its ranks and that they are working with slayers to remove us, right? They claim vampires do not follow orders and that we are self-serving in our actions. They say we put personal goals ahead of the CIA's goals." I wanted to ask the questions with force. I wanted to demand her answers, but I sounded weak, like I was begging her to answer.

Nelson moved away from the laptop and bed and took his turn looking out the window into the daylight. "The CIA is right; my goals will never include taking organs from children" was his proclamation.

"I kept looking," Natalie said. "This morning and now, but after the children arrived at the facilities there are no records of them leaving, none. And the sad truth is, there is no indication that the children actually made it to the facilities. Organs are housed in the centers. Maybe those sixteen suffocated were supposed to die inside that freight car. I think the error was them being discovered."

She was labeling the railway car as a death car. An extermination trap for the children.

"No." Nelson almost pleaded.

A nurse entered and brought me water and three pills; I

took both from her and asked, "Where am I?"

She looked to Charlette before answering; Charlette nodded yes.

"The Metropolitan Correctional Center in Chicago, on the medical floor."

I took the pills, drank the water from the small cup, and gave it back to her.

"Thank you."

The nurse left without saying another word.

"Are we under arrest?" I asked Charlette.

"Not really, but yes" was her answer.

"Who is holding us?"

"The CIA, Pike." She answered my question, but her glance was out the window.

"We're leaving." I wanted to stand for emphasis, but standing was not happening; my legs didn't have the needed push to rise from the chair. I could not summon the strength.

"You can't. From what I understand, you are all considered dangers to the State." Her eyes went from the window to me, and she quickly winked her eye at me, and that ... confused the hell out me.

CHAPTER
- SIXTEEN -

His name was Jackson Hampton, and he refused to join the family of the vampire who gave him the gift. The vampire that bit him was destroyed by slayers while waiting for Jackson to wake after he bit him. The family was taken over by the eldest male, who Jackson refused to follow.

Jackson told whoever would listen that the living-death was a curse and vampires were an abomination. He told me he hated being a vampire, but he had existed for over a hundred and fifty years as a vampire. He was given the living-death when he was nineteen years old, and the night our friendship began he was driving a silver Bentley coupe.

I was crossing the street at 87th and Stony Island going east. He was heading north. When I looked into the car, I recognized him. He had celebrity status as a bad boy vampire, an outlaw not belonging to any family. He knew me and my family. We smiled at each other, and I kept walking. He made the turn heading east and parked two blocks ahead of me. He jogged back to me and joined me walking.

He began with, "I spoke with Daniel last night."

It was probably my second year of existing as a vampire, and I could have counted on one hand the number of vampires outside the family that told me they had spoken with Daniel. So, him saying that was really out of the norm.

"Really, about what?"

He seemed a fast walker, but he slowed himself to my pace.

"What?" he asked, grinning.

"What did you speak to Daniel about?"

He was about a foot taller than me, so him looking me in my face required some effort, but he did it. "Ok, you caught me. I didn't speak to him. I just figured it would be a good way to break the ice."

"By lying?" I was walking at a nice pace, and I purposely didn't break stride to see his expression.

"Ok, maybe not so good. What are you doing walking down the street?"

There were a good number of people out enjoying the late evening air.

"I like walking."

The area was busy with commerce; shops remained open to around nine, and plenty of people walked down 87th Street and Stony Island Avenue.

"And I like the night air and the people. I enjoy people watching."

A young man zoomed between us on a skateboard

balancing a pizza.

"See, you don't see that every day."

He laughed. "I do see that every day." He watched the boy making it through the crowd. "Are you looking to feed?"

I had fed the previous night off of a police officer robbing a young man who was selling weed.

"No. I'm just out walking."

"I don't feed off of humans." I felt him looking down at me to see how I responded. I didn't look up.

"I've heard."

"Have you now? What else have you heard?"

We paused because a silver metallic Chevy Impala was blocking the crosswalk; the driver burned rubber pealing onto 87th Street heading west. He waited for my response.

"I heard you own a logistics company, and you hunt down deer and wolves and coyotes to feed. I also heard you hate being a vampire, but you have existed as one for a hundred plus years."

Since we were not walking, I looked up at him. He was a very handsome man. "You look like Thelonious Monk."

He smiled again, "I've heard that before. You like jazz?"

Me listening to Jazz was recent. "It has grown on me; Daniel started me listening to it. I heard you play the piano."

His smile stretched into a grin. "It seems you have heard quite a bit about me, and most of it seems accurate. However, I don't hunt down animals. I am against killing anything. When I was human, I was a vegan."

We restarted our walk and crossed the street.

We stopped at his car.

"Hey, I was going downtown to watch the boats for Venetian Night, you want to join me? There are a lot of people and boats to watch." He opened his car door for me, smiling.

* * *

When we pulled up to the Yacht Club, the attendants came out and parked Jackson's car, and they escorted us to seats on a floating stage. The stage was pulled out onto the lake with rowboats, and it was positioned so the boats participating in Venetian Night passed right by us on both sides. The event was breathtaking.

I asked him, "Is this a cursed life?"

Watching the candlelit boats passing, he answered, "If I would have lived it as others directed me, then yes, this existence would have been cursed. I made being a vampire fit my beliefs as best I could; there are realities that plague me, but that is a conversation for another night."

I could tell he wanted to enjoy the evening and not discuss the merits of vampirism, but I had one more question.

"Do you wish you were still human?"

"Every minute and every second of every day. The wealth I have, I would have gotten as a human. I was an extremely aggressive and motivated person."

I thought about his words, aggressive and motivated. I had accomplished little as a human. I was a confused student thinking of dropping out and was on the verge of being fired from my telemarketing job when I met Christopher. He was aggressive and motivated. He had goals and plans, and he helped me to see how important goals were. We set goals together, and I began to feel the excitement of accomplishing goals, the joy of plans coming to fruition, but then they killed him.

"I was not aggressive or motivated. I was suicidal. So, the living-death changed everything for me."

"Your mind, your thinking, might have changed over time."

My thinking had changed due to Christopher, but when he was murdered everything went gray.

"No, had Daniel not removed the pills from my palm, I would have died by my own hand."

I looked from the boats to him. He was not looking at the boats. He was thoughtfully considering my words.

"I am so very happy you are here."

* * *

While lying naked in his penthouse bed and looking into his face, I was resting on an extremely long and fluffy pillow, and I saw a very perplexed look on his face, and I knew its origin. Our having sex had required him to be very patient. He was trying to figure out how to ask about the difficulty he experienced.

He finally asked, "So, you were a virgin when you were given the gift?"

Being a virgin was important to me as a human. I wanted to share myself with a man I would love for life. That man died. As a vampire, I just wanted to do it.

"Yes, I was given the gift on my wedding night."

I could tell he wanted to ask me why him, and why that night. And I really did not have a reason. I had no extreme emotional attachments to him; the opportunity presented itself to have sex, and I took it. If I would have never saw Jackson Hampton again, it would have been ok with me.

"The only other virgin I slept was my high school girlfriend, and she loved me."

His face had a curious, probing expression; as if he was

asking if I loved him.

I almost laughed out loud, so I quickly answered, "I don't love you."

His face relaxed with relief.

"I didn't think you did."

Neither of us moved our heads from the fluffy pillows.

We had sex five more times that year; he always took me to some fantastic event: NBA Playoffs, a lunar eclipse, the birth of lion cubs, an Elton John concert in London, and the filming of an Oprah Christmas show. But the last time I saw him was not sexual. He'd come to see me at Daniel's.

We were in the living room alone sitting on the sofa, and Daniel, who was in the kitchen, was constantly questioning me in my head: "What does that outlaw want with you? Why is he here? How long have you known him?" I did not answer one of his queries.

What Jackson wanted surprised me. He had a logistics company, Pirate International, which he used to support his biological family.

"I don't have many friends; none really, and I don't trust any vampire other than you. This business is not linked to any other vampire-owned companies, but I bank wholly with vampire-owned institutions, so it is not unknown. And as you know, I have not aligned with any family, and if something was to happen to me none of my wealth would be delegated to my human biological family. Vampires will devour all I have. So, I am leaving everything to you with the stipulation that you continue to provide for my biological family as I have done. I cannot put the stipulation in writing, so the agreement is between you and me as friends."

We had become friends, so I agreed, and I signed the papers. I was expecting us to leave and seal the deal in sex, but he merely kissed me goodnight and left. The next night we found out that he had walked into the sunlight in front of a church.

- Sunday -

Four suited agents abruptly entered the hospital room. One confiscated the laptop from the bed and left, and the other three stood in opposing corners of the room. The agents were followed by Director Pike, Jocelyn, and Detective Moss. Pike and Charlette nodded to each other, and she left the room.

Pike, a massive human being, reminded me of a silverback gorilla. He was taller and wider and darker than everyone in the room. His eyes were dark brown, but they were lighter than his skin, which gave him an odd look. His dark brown eyes, lighter than his skin, were on me.

"Tell me, how does it feel to be human again? Fantastic, huh? You should have thanked your sister instead of attacking her." He wasn't smiling, and it sounded a lot like he was giving me orders.

He must have heard our whole conversation, and the laptop Charlette gave Natalie probably captured my cloud log-in information. Pike adjusted his gold necktie and grinned at me.

"You hacked my computer. I guess, I left too many hints. Do you know how many log-in passwords I have? You wouldn't believe me if I told you." He looked at me as if I was going to guess.

My response was to mean mug him. I'd met with Pike three times before; he was rude, he was condescending, he made assumptions, and he was a bully.

"I understand being pissed; those vampire powers were boss. But now, you are back to being a human slug. Dragging your knuckles through the mud with the rest of us primates; but never fear, you all still got your good CIA jobs."

Suddenly, Natalie spewed out "Bitch!" and leapt towards Jocelyn, but the suited agent closest to her restrained her as the well-trained professional he was. He had one hand on her shoulder and his other hand curved her arm behind her back. Her advance was immediately stopped.

Jocelyn chuckled, "I was doing my job, relax. We are all on the same team now." She hunched her shoulders and tilted her head, smiling at my daughter.

I hadn't trusted Jocelyn, but I didn't make her out to be CIA. However, her actions supported what she was; her acceptance of me as a vampire and her joining us with little regard to leaving her life should have been warning signs. She was good at deception.

"And what about you, slayer?" I snarled at Moss, whose disgust-filled gaze was heavy on me.

"Oh, me," he nodded his head. "I still hate your demon ass, and the only thing that is stopping me from putting a bullet in your head is the CIA."

I believed every word he said because I still hated his ass. It wasn't over; my plans still included taking Moss's head and Pike's head.

Pike released a guttural grunt and looked toward the window, then his eyes perused the room. "Please, kiddies, let's put all this pointless misdirected angry aside. We need to clear some things up." He took a couple of steps toward the bed and stopped at the foot of it. Again, he looked at everyone in the room, even the suited agents. He told the agent holding Natalie, "Release her," which he did.

Pike put his eyes directly on me. "As vampires, you were all CIA consultants. I have contracts with each of you. However, as humans, who wish to keep the considerable wealth you obtained as vampires ... you need to become CIA agents. Every one of you."

He paused for effect. I looked to Nelson and Natalie, and neither looked like they were going to refuse the offer.

"If, by some strange flaw in your logic, you find this unacceptable, one of these men will put a .9mm slug in your brain, right now."

Again, he paused for effect and looked at each of us.

"As humans, all of you are already dead. What I'm offering is a life, a human life with your vampire names and money." He didn't wait for a reply. "There is a car waiting to drive you to a facility where you will be given your mission updates. Agent Jocelyn Warren is the mission lead."

Detective Moss took steps directed toward me, and I wanted to stand, but before I could gather the strength to move, he spat down into my face.

"That was for my partner."

He quickly drew my dagger from his suit coat and lunged at me. I sprung up from the chair with every ounce of strength I had. My hands were around his neck and my force was backing him up, but I heard two zips, and Detective Moss collapsed to the floor, getting freed from my grip.

His face was bleeding, a lot. I looked behind me and saw two bullets holes in the small whiteboard with my name and vitals on it. Those bullets, the bullets that went through Moss's head, could have just as easily gone into my head.

Pike could have killed us both.

I looked down again at Moss and saw my dagger. I lowered to him by bending my stiff knees and retrieved my dagger.

"Stupid fucker." Director Pike holstered his silenced pistol. "I need you more than I needed him, Melody Knight." He stood above Moss's corpse, shaking his head to the negative. "All of you, put your past behind you if you want to live. What is at stake here is larger than your petty ass vengeance."

One of the suits began talking as if he was on a radio. "Immediate clean up. Slayer protocol, the Metropolitan Correctional Center, medical floor. Authorization, Pike 1414."

I was standing and breathing heavy. I had energy, angry energy, and it felt good.

CHAPTER
- SEVENTEEN -

My biological dad died about four years after Daniel gave me the gift of the living-death. I had gone to Atlanta to see how they were responding to the influx of cash that I was cleverly sending their way. When I arrived, their shoe shop was draped in a purple and black funeral cloth. I entered their home as gas; his funeral repast was occurring.

My mother was being consoled by her sister and my father's brother. There were a lot of family and friends present. She was in good hands. Grief and sadness were not often felt as a vampire. I cannot remember experiencing any emotion that changed my behavior, as emotions did when I was human. Things made me smile as a vampire, but I was not filled with joy. I did get agitated, but I seldom raged in anger.

I accepted my father's death, and I was satisfied that my mother's finances were in order, so I left. There was nothing else for me to do. The practicality of being a vampire agreed with my thinking. When Jackson Hampton walked into the sunlight in front of that church, I didn't mourn his loss. I went to the lawyers and bankers associated with his company, Pirate International, and stepped in as CEO and owner.

Having a corporation made sending funds to my mother easier; I followed the example Jackson used to send support to his human family. I experienced pleasure from being successful within the competitive structure of corporate America, but there was no passion, no obsession to succeed. I expected to win, and I did. Humans were slow and easily surpassed.

- Sunday -

We were escorted from the Metropolitan Correctional Center in Chicago to a black SUV and driven less than three miles away to a two-story warehouse. The warehouse was in the middle of the Lincoln Park neighborhood on an artsy block. I had gone to the art gallery next door many times, and the used bookstore on the other side of the warehouse was one of my favorites. I always thought the warehouse was a furniture company.

The door opened though retina recognition. I watched the laser scan Pike's eyes, and he had to place his palm against a screen that uncovered after the retina scan. Once inside, we instantly saw it was not a warehouse.

The walls and the lowered ceilings were stark white.

Florescent lights ran through the offices. Scattered people dressed in formal business attire stepped briskly through the areas. No one looked in our direction. We followed Pike towards a large two-person reception desk. The floors were carpeted with a brown and mauve blend. We stepped into a horseshoe reception area; the large reception desk had two suited agent types at each end. Neither Pike nor the other agents with us spoke to the two. No nods of the heads or any type of office pleasantry was exchanged.

To the left and right of the desk were pairs of mahogany wood doors. Behind the desk was a cast-iron staircase leading to the second floor. I watched the hurried passerby, but again, no one spoke.

Pike progressed to the mahogany doors to the left. We followed him through the doors into a large meeting room. Sitting at the conference table were Charlette, Thomas Adomako, and his mother, Tina Adomako. She was as human as the rest of us. They both smiled and rose from the chairs and came to me. We three embraced and Natalie joined us in the hug exchange.

"They broke into my home, assaulted me with a steam that stripped me of all my powers, dragged me out of my bed, and threw me on a plane like a sack of yams. But, praise God, I am here now with my two favorite people in the world. God is good."

I had to hug her again.

Pike ignored our reunion and went to the head of the conference table. He placed his palm down on the table and a keyboard appeared within the table in front of him. The room darkened, and we all took seats. The wall behind Pike became a screen. The face of Fernando Castillo was present.

"This man was our inroad to the financing behind what

you think you have discovered." Pike wasn't looking at the screen behind him. He was looking down at a screen. He slid his finger across the screen in the table, and the picture behind him changed. "We have linked Banco Republica to the orphanages and Rollins Transportation."

Natalie interrupted him with, "The orphanages – you are kidding, right? You bastards are paying the directors' salaries through Rollins Transportation."

Pike didn't bother to look up to answer. "You have it wrong. Rollins Transportation is not the CIA."

"Bullshit," was Natalie's loud response.

I wanted her to shut up because Pike was an unpredicttable killer. He might have shot her for interrupting him.

"No. We were tracking the actions of Rollins; we watched their money flow; and like you, we summarized it was company doing more than transporting freight. But unlike you, we didn't jump to conclusions without facts. Banco Republica is now the sole owner of Rollins Transportation. And if you would have dug a little deeper, you would have discovered the link between Rollins, Banco Republica, and the eight orphanages. Castillo was the link between all three, and we had developed enough intel to direct his actions, but our vampire consultant took it upon herself to kill the asset."

If he looked in my direction, the darkness of the room hid his glance. An image of Banco Republica appeared on the screen, but it wasn't the one in Cuba. He showed the one in Rome, then Madrid, then Mexico, then Venice, then Istanbul, then Moscow, and finally New York.

"The corporation that is Banco Republica has established interest, no ... they have established global domination of the human organ market."

A newspaper article appeared on the screen. It was written by Thomas Adomako. It was titled, "The Next Gold Rush." A blue light illuminated Thomas. His eyes blinked, showing his surprise.

"Tell them what you uncovered," Pike ordered. "Perhaps your godmother and the others will listen to you."

Only Thomas's face and upper torso could be seen in the room. He cleared his throat and began. "My reporting did not involve Banco Republica, so this is news to me. And it is information I would be quite interested in hearing more about. My brief work is associated with two relatively small companies that have cornered the human organ market.

"They appear able to meet the demands of the market with an agility that formal nations with many citizens are unable to meet. It appears if a patient, a customer, has the funds, the needed organ can be immediately supplied in sixteen hours.

"At one time, each small company operated out of a single site, and each depended heavily on Legacy Transportation. My reporting revealed that eventually the two companies became Legacy Transportation's only customers. The two companies combined have only twenty-three locations, which makes their supply capabilities impossible. My reporting ends with a question: How are they doing it? How are they successfully meeting the demand?"

The blue light faded from Thomas. We were all sitting in darkness when Pike said, "Two demands: supply – the actual organs – and delivery. How are they delivering organs within sixteen hours all across the world? That is humanly impossible, no?"

The blue light spotlighted Tina, who blinked in surprise. Pike directed, "Tell us about your business with Rollins

Transportation."

Tina brought her thumb and forefinger to her chin. Her eyes were focused straight ahead. The room had to be dark for her as it was for the rest us, but she seemed to be looking at something.

"Maybe six or seven years ago, I was approached by a Rollins Plasma. We – Marcus and I – helped them establish a plasma delivery service. I have tweaked it for them over the years because of growth, mostly logistics problems, but they pay well so finding contractors is not a problem. I helped them establish relationships with plasma collection centers across the globe. It took some work in the beginning, but now they have capable management. My consultation is limited at present; maybe three or four times a year. But even in the beginning, they didn't require much attention."

She was still encompassed by the blue light when Pike asked, "Capable management? You mean vampires and minions, right?"

The face of Alvin Shore appeared on the screen.

"Yes, the management I met were vampires and minions."

"Who is that on the screen?"

"The president of Rollins Plasma, Alvin Shore."

"Vampire?"

"Yes."

"Not anymore," Nelson said quietly.

The blue light faded from Tina. The only light in the room was being emitted from Alvin Shore's face.

The light shined from the rim of the conference table to Nelson Shore, illuminating his face and torso. His eyes blinked as well.

"Tell us about Rollins Transportation."

Nelson didn't hesitate. "It was my dad's company. He and Daniel Knight started it a century and a half ago. It started as a railroad company. I never worked with them, but my brother did."

Jocelyn cleared her throat in the darkness. "Correction, your brother does work with them," and the room was flooded with florescent light, which brought closed eyes and groans throughout the room.

Pike laughed out loud at our discomfort. Unaffected, he continued on the screen in front of him within the table. The large screen behind him took on a whiteboard format, and Jocelyn stood and walked to it. Pike sat in the chair at the head of the table.

Standing at the whiteboard, Jocelyn wrote out names I recognized, Jenkins Holdings and Pristine Medical.

"These companies were small businesses with loans from Banco Republica. After we tried to redirect their business trajectory, the corporation of Banco Republica took them over. Perhaps our involvement brought them to their attention, who knows. But once they were officially under the corporate umbrella of Banco Republica, they grew, and they expanded. We know of twenty-three official distribution sites, but when we add the plasma centers operated by Rollins, those numbers multiply into the thousands." She wrote out 8117, "to be exact."

Charlette raised her hand and asked, "What are you saying, that vampires and Banco Republica are killing children and selling their organs?"

No one answered her.

Pike asked, "Is that so hard to believe? Is it easier to believe that the CIA is killing orphans and selling their organs? But it is not just children. The vampire involvement expands their donor market; yes, they are still using the children, but intelligence has shown tens of thousands of adult humans have been used as organ donors."

I moved my eyes to Charlette and told her, "I find it hard to believe that my father would be involved with children dying or the selling of human organs for profit."

Charlette nodded her head in the affirmative, "So do I."

"A hundred and fifty-year-old company does change focus. As founders, their influence in the day-to-day was probably minimal," Natalie offered.

"I agree" came from Nelson. "My dad talked a lot about what the company was, and the battles he and Daniel faced and overcame. I seldom heard or observed conversations between he and Alvin about current business situations; it was a lot like he was retired."

Pike waved Jocelyn away from the whiteboard. He stood from his chair and cleared the board.

"I really don't give a rats ass about who you think would do what. Fuck the past. I cannot be any clearer than that. I want Rollins Transportation and Banco Republica's organ donor business in the hands of CIA operatives. I want those orphanages cleaned up or wiped from the face of the earth.

"Slayers have been directed to attack the vampire and minion managers at Rollins, so the company should be in turmoil as we speak. We have a detailed plan of action which Joycelyn will share with you individually. There are cabs waiting outside to take you to your homes and to the airport. You will meet with Joycelyn within forty-eight hours for individual assignments. Now get the fuck out."

I didn't move. "When you say being attacked, are you destroying vampires?" I asked Pike, but my glance was going back and forth between him and Charlette.

"Those that we need will be converted, and the others will be destroyed." His answer was stated dryly, and Charlette refused to make eye contact with me. "They have been using human donors to supply a global enterprise. Fuck vampires."

I told him, "You will start a war. A war between vampires and humans."

"The war has been started; we are just becoming aware. Vampires are using humans to supply other humans with organs. The commodities are fighting back."

CHAPTER
- EIGHTEEN -

"Has anyone ever told you that you are self-centered?" He asked as we walked along the Atlantic City Boardwalk on a star-filled night; it was a night that followed a horrific storm less than two hours before. It was only he and I on the wooden boardwalk, and the waves were still high.

"People have told me I was spoiled; is that what you are asking?"

"No, I think only psychopaths are spoiled. Spoiled implies rotten, no redemption. Self-centered means your focus is entirely or mostly on your own wants and desires."

"And that's a bad thing?"

"A balanced person is able to find value in helping others, and all their actions are not self-gratifying. Achieving personal goals should be balanced with helping others; that

is what makes one balanced."

"And why is being balanced desired? There are things I want to do for me; my concerns are about me. My energy is used getting what I want. What is unbalanced about that?"

I heard the waves, and I wanted to stop and look at them, but Daniel kept walking and talking.

"You are part of this family, my family. You do things to help others in it: you drove Charlette to the airport, you helped Juanita with investments. And this family, your family, is part of a larger vampire family; we are in business with other families. We bank with vampire-owned banks. We help our vampire community.

"And our community moves beyond vampires. We share this country with humans; vampires have fought wars with Americans; we have assisted them in fighting diseases, in financial crises, and in times of natural disasters. We work with the CIA and the FBI out of concern for the country.

"If you only did things that helped you, you would be of no help to your sisters or Alexander or me. The family would be out of balance because you helped no one but yourself; we would be helping you, but you would not be helping us ... creating an imbalance.

"If we Knights continued to earn our wealth independently and did not partner with any other vampire families, our community would suffer from a lack of shared resources. When prosperity is shared, the whole community benefits. The help we give today is returned during a troubled tomorrow. When we help humans, the country prospers, and a prosperous country increases the population. All relationships require balance; a give-and-take is necessary for any relationship to work.

"For a person to be in a relationship with others that

person must be balanced; one cannot only receive, one cannot only work on selfish concerns, one's focus cannot stay on one's self, not while maintaining functioning relationships; there must be balance."

"So how am I self-centered?"

"You inherited Pirate International from a very self-centered vampire. One who not only refused to join a family, but who would work with other vampires only in service: banks and lawyers that provided him a service. He had no partners and shared no wealth. And you are doing the same."

I wanted to pause, but Daniel kept walking. Jackson had given the company to me. I didn't see the need to involve others. We both used it to support our human families in secret. He didn't involve other vampires and neither did I.

"And this was not an observation I made; it was brought to my attention by other vampires."

"Sounds like jealously to me."

"Perhaps, but valid nonetheless. You are a Knight, and your actions reflect upon me."

"Wow, that sounds kind of self-centered to me."

He laughed and continued to walk.

- Monday -

The damage to my home had been expertly repaired, and it had been professionally cleaned. There were no bits of broken glass, no drywall residue, no splinters of anything; it was as if the raid only happened in my mind. Nothing was out of place; missing was the dagger I took from the stand after the slayer attack, my phone, and my laptop. Thankfully,

Moss inadvertently brought the dagger back to me. I placed it back in its stand and sat at my desk. Natalie sat on the daybed and Nelson collapsed into my wicker chair.

"How long before the CIA meets with us?" he asked.

"I expect Jocelyn this morning. We are the worker bees; the plan was probably built around us," I answered.

"Yeah, you're right, Mother. They need us, and that Pike is a heartless demon. We will be put to work immediately."

Nelson extended his feet and looked down at his boots as if he wanted to take them off. He moved his eyes to Natalie and challenged with, "No, I disagree. He sees the reality of the situation. It's just business."

Her objection to his words showed in her wrinkled forehead. She asked him, "How do you figure that?"

Nelson pulled the laces on each boot to untie them, but he didn't remove them.

"Rollins Transportation and Banco Republica have taken over a vital market. A market America feels it should control, and they took over that market using human orphans and human adults from across the world with vampire help. What did he call humans – commodities? People are commodities in a vampire-controlled market, and Pike's job is to take over the market and put it in American hands."

If my daughter had still been a vampire, the conversation would have been over because she would have swooshed out of the room. Being held in the room and in the conversation, she queried, "What about the vampire deaths that will occur from the takeover?"

Nelson removed his boots with his feet; using the opposite foot to remove the other. Natalie challenging didn't raise any ire or obvious irritation from Nelson. He spoke matter-of-factly.

"What about the human deaths that occurred with them developing control of the market? It's all business, and in this business, humans are commodities, and they have been expendable, and for the market to change hands vampires will be expendable."

Natalie stood erect from the daybed and asked, "And you are ok with that?"

Nelson crossed his blue, socked-covered ankles. "What choice do I have? I am human, and so are you and your mother. That is our reality. We are human CIA agents who have been given the opportunity to keep our vampire wealth."

Natalie dropped back down to sitting and cocked her head to a curious puppy angle. "But your brother may be part of the annihilation?"

Shaking his head no, Nelson declared, "Not if I'm involved, which I am. I have to see the positive if I am going to survive. Yes, vampires will die, but some will be converted to humans like we were."

I understood his words. He was accepting the change and being practical in his thinking. The front doorbell chimed, signaling an internal visitor. I wasn't surprised and neither was my daughter or Nelson.

I nodded at Nelson, and he stood and went to the door. When he opened the door, Jocelyn walked right in as if she was at home. With a briefcase in hand, she came directly to my office and sat in the wicker chair Nelson left empty.

"Good morning, agents."

She placed the briefcase on the floor and flipped it open and retrieved a manilla folder. She was dressed in casual business attire: beige khakis and a peach polo.

Nelson sat on the floor in front of the daybed next to Natalie.

"Melody, the assignment is similar to others you have done."

"A kill target?" I asked.

"Multiple targets; one for each of you. You, Natalie, and Nelson will form a unit with my lead."

She pulled photographs out of the briefcase, stood from the wicker chair, and passed a group of three out to each of us.

"There is a software convention being held here; actually, we, the CIA, organized and formed the convention seven months ago to get the targets here. You all would have been assigned one of these targets independently through Chad or your handler. I guess that makes me the new Chad." She alone laughed at her joke, and she remained standing over us.

"The targets are either logistics engineers or senior vice presidents at Rollins Transportation or Banco Republica; their deaths will bring chaos, two from Rollins and one from Republica. We want each administered the same poison. It kills within ten minutes, once it is in the bloodstream, and there is no antidote."

She bent down to the case and pulled three pen cases from it.

"We want the targets to die on stage while they are speaking as leaders of their corporations. That means the poison must not be applied too early. Understand?"

She looked at each of us sternly, and that pissed me off. Anger was a consistent emotion for me as a human. Jocelyn handed us each a pen case. While holding the case, I saw my hand fade to a gaseous state. I had to catch the case with my flesh hand before it fell.

"These pens will project five doses through needle-thin darts. It only takes one to bring death, but more than one will not speed up the ingestion process, so if you need more than one attempt, it is ok. However, be extremely careful; you are no longer vampires, so these darts will kill you.

"The panel they are speaking on begins at 7 p.m. They are all featured guests dining at the same table in front of the stage. All of you are waitstaff; I will be there working as well. You are to arrive at the convention center at 5 p.m.; there will be waitstaff work to do." Again, she gave each of us a stern look.

But my hand turning gaseous had my attention. When I looked down again, the hand was flesh.

Natalie asked her, "And what makes you think that one of us won't dart you?"

Jocelyn sat back down in my wicker chair. She smiled a warm smile, a concerned smile. "Because, no matter what comes out of your mouths, each of you want these lives back, and I don't think fucking them up is part of your agendas. If you kill me, those lives are screwed. I cannot imagine how it feels to have the type of financial security each of you have. But I imagine that losing it would be earth-shattering."

My desk phone chirped; it was the front desk.

"That would be your sister."

I answered the phone.

"There is a Ms. Charlette Knight to see you, Ms. Knight?"

"Let her up."

I stood from my desk because I wanted to be the one to let Charlette in.

"She will have a nurse with her; you all have to be

checked: vitals and conversion stability, not there is a real concern, just checking."

My hand fading made me nervous as I walked by Jocelyn. I didn't want her to witness the fading before I understood it. Fortunately, everything remained stable on my walk to the door. Jocelyn had it wrong; I didn't value human life more than vampire life. I would rather be a poor vampire than a rich human. A vampire had power and power generated opportunities.

The nurse walked in before Charlette. I recognized her from the MCCC ward. I pointed to the office area, and she headed in that direction. Charlette and I paused at the door.

"Well?" she asked, looking me in my eyes.

I didn't look away.

"Why didn't you tell us about the weapon?"

"Because the conversion device wasn't designed to be a weapon, and both of you wanted to stay vampires. You two never listened to me."

"Did you spray Juanita?"

"No, if I had she'd be alive. I was trying to save you both. She didn't have to die."

"But she did."

Unexpectedly, I started crying and so did Charlette. We hugged each other and spent moments crying together. We cried for Daniel, and we cried for Juanita, and we cried because things had changed, forever.

In my ear, she whispered, "Are you going to kill Pike?"

Her question didn't surprise me, it disappointed me; she didn't ask are "we" going to kill Pike. I broke our embrace and walked to the mirror.

"I haven't seen myself in thirty plus years, and I look exactly how I remember, well ... better, actually."

We laughed.

"I know. Seeing yourself is freaky, right?"

Despite the shared laugh, Charlette's question about Pike circled in my mind. Was I going to kill him? Could I kill him as a human? And why did she assume she was safe from my wrath?

Still looking in the mirror, I told her, "You and the CIA took something from me; you took the gift my father gave me. But you returned something as well. You gave me back my humanity. I'm not sure about Pike yet. Why?"

Charlette came and stood behind me. Both of our reflections were in the mirror.

"Because ... I'm not sure either. He promised me Juanita would be safe, and I'm not certain of his involvement with Daniel's death. He has done so much for me and my research. But ... he speaks so easily of killing others." She lowered her eyes. "I'm just not sure anymore."

It was easy for me to believe her because she was my sister, and I saw her tears and her confusion in the mirror. Then we both saw the reflection of my face fading. I faded out completely. I returned slightly but faded again. Charlette stopped crying. She was smiling, and she winked at me again. I was gone from the mirror, and I felt the power surging through me. I heard Jocelyn saying "Oh, shit." She was reaching for the case. I swooshed from my home through the kitchen sink pipes that led down to the basement and into the pipes that led to the sewers.

CHAPTER
- NINETEEN -

We were strolling the boardwalk and Daniel paused, then stopped and looked out to the ocean. "These waves make me think of my origins. My beginnings."

It was my fourth year being his daughter and that was his first mention of his beginning, so I said nothing and listened.

He saw me listening intently and chuckled. "Each of my daughters has done the same; each of you have waited for me to tell my story. I wonder why none of you asked. Funny. Did you ask one of the others?"

"No." I hadn't, and neither of them brought the conversation to me; it was strange. We stood facing the ocean.

"The year was 1623, and our village was attacked by what I thought were ghost warriors: men with white skin, rifles, and metal swords. I saw my father killed. I fought, but I was overpowered, tied, and bound into a line of others. The white warriors walked us day and night to the coast.

We stayed on the shore docks bound to one another for what seemed like weeks. They fed us like livestock out of buckets and troths. It was the worst I had ever lived ... until that ship arrived. If there is hell, it cannot be worse than the ship that brought us to Virginia.

While in the belly of the ship, I saw men and women held so firmly by despair that they willed their own deaths. I saw groups of ten, fifteen chained people act as one and jump overboard to their deaths. We were all physically sick on the ship: fever, vomiting, loose stool, collapsing, seizures, and death were constants. We should have all died, but we didn't, and when the ship finally docked, I was certain we were in hell because all the people were white like those on the ship and those that attacked our village.

"After my fear subsided, I recognized market business happening all around us, and I kept hearing the word Virginia, so I thought Virginia meant market. We all were on our knees in the sand, and they kept taking people out of the chained lines to wagons. We figured out that people were being sold with horses, wagons, plows, and sacks of seeds.

"I couldn't figure out how or when we were being sold, but I was yanked from the line still chained and thrown into a wagon with five others. We were taken to a tobacco plantation. Wade was the plantation owner's name. He was British and his wife was Dutch. The labor was intense, and we worked from sunup to sundown. After a year, I escaped with two others when Powhatan warriors attacked the planation.

"One of the two plantation slaves was native to the land,

and the other African, and I followed them through the woods to a body of water. There was an island seen through the dusk sky. The native left us when darkness came. We lay on the ground waiting for morning. When the sun rose, we swam to the island. We found campfire ash, clothes, weapons, and other signs of people, but no people. We searched all of the small island but found no one. We caught some fish, made a fire, and ate well. When nightfall came, we were on the menu.

"Vampires rose up out the dark water that was surrounding the island. They appeared to be walking across the water to the island shore. Their attack was swift, and we were both given the living-death. We were bitten by Africans from Dahomey, and they had a plan.

"Yimwen, the one who gave me the gift, told me, 'We are returning home; this land is not for us. We will travel through the night and go under the sea in the day. We are going home. We will follow the east star by night.'

"He was talking about Venus." Daniel pointed to the planet. "Their plan was to swoosh back to Africa one night at a time, and he swooshed around the island to demonstrate the practicality of the plan. We were amazed by the swooshing, and he taught us how to swoosh that very night. He and the others had been staying under water around the island in the day and feeding at night. They had gone on the mainland and given over twenty Africans the gift of the living-death. The majority of those they had given the gift to joined them on the island, and they were willing to attempt the trip back to Africa. I was willing.

"But Justin was not. He told me, 'At home, we will be the walking dead, we will be shunned by all. You know this. We will be returning to persecution, not home. They will see us as unclean.' He was right, and I knew it, but so did others and they were willing to try and return.

"Justin told me, 'I am going to kill those that brought me here, those who took me from my home.' His anger was understood, but those people, white people, were all around us. The thought of returning home seemed the safer task.

"I didn't think they could make it back to Africa by swooshing and walking under the sea, but I was willing to try; being a slave was not the life I wanted, but I didn't want to be a vampire either. None of the options before me was acceptable. Justin said, 'We will not be slaves here. We will be lions, and those white people will be our goats.'

"His words made me smile. Yimwen saw my smile.

He shook his head, no, but I couldn't hold back the smile that morphed into a grin. Justin was right; the thought of revenge surged through me. I thought about my father, and I thought about those who died in the belly of that ship and those that jumped overboard. Bringing death to the whites seemed acceptable.

"I looked at Yimwen and told him, my friend is correct, the battle is here on these lands. Justin yelled, 'I will rule this world with the power you gave me.' And he took flight and swooshed to the mainland, and I followed.

"We ravished the first planation we saw, killing every white person present. We knew how to kill, but we did not know how to feed, so we ate more flesh than we drank blood. We were vengeful beasts. We hid in caves during the day and brought destruction and death to settlement sites and plantations nightly.

"Although we didn't know it, we were being watched but not approached."

- Monday -

When I emerged from Calvin Melrose's sewer pipes, I expected the basement to be empty, but on the floor were two dead white-eyed slayers and a seriously wounded Calvin. I took the sword from his hand and sliced my palm open. My blood was vampire green. I made a fist and my blood dipped onto his lips; he opened his mouth and my blood filled it. The wounds across his shoulder and chest healed instantly. His eyes brightened. He looked up at me confused and sat erect.

"They told me you were human, Sister Melody; they came here with CIA agents demanding information; I told them nothing. They dragged me down here to kill me, but I fought them. I was fighting to my death. I would never betray you, Sister."

"I know."

"You are not human?"

"I was, but it didn't take." I couldn't stop the grin. "They used a weapon on me, but the human effects didn't last."

There was a thermos on the ledge of the concrete sink. I got it from the sink and took the top off and filled half the top with my blood, which Calvin drank.

"The CIA agents called for that weapon, and they wanted to wait for it; the plan was to use it on me, but the slayers decided they wanted to battle me hand-to-hand. They said I had a reputation as a great warrior among slayers. They brought me down here and foolishly allowed me to pick a weapon." He pointed to their corpses and grinned. "They should have listened to the rumors. I don't know if the agents are still upstairs or not."

He stood, stretching his massive body up toward the

basement ceiling; his joints creaked and popped.

"They're not," I told him. "The café is empty."

He went to the stairs and climbed them. I heard a phone buzzing and went through one of the slayers' pants pockets. The text message played in audio; it was requesting a check in; more slayers would raid the café soon.

I yelled to Calvin, "Go get your car, slayers are on the way."

He left and I heard the door locking behind him. I needed his help, and I needed vampire help. I pulled Justin Shore's home number from my memory. I doubted it would be any good after the raid, but I dialed it anyway.

He answered, "Hello."

"Justin?"

"Melody. Where are you?"

"You were wrong; they changed me to human, but I changed back."

He chuckled. "Good, and your power?"

"I never felt stronger. I need your help."

Climbing the stairs, I saw my naked thigh.

"Anything you need, Melody. My son?"

"He is human."

I went back down the stairs and pulled a gold Nike tracksuit and black running shoes from the metal wardrobe.

"I'm going to rent a suite at the Hyatt; I need you to meet me there in an hour and bring help."

He hadn't said a word since I told him Nelson was human. The man had lost three sons in less than twenty-four hours. I dressed quickly and sped up the stairs to Calvin's desk.

Justin Shore asked, "How much help will you need?"

"Three other vampires and if you can ... get them from

three different families."

"No problem."

I ended the call sitting at Calvin's desk with a clear view of the front door. Two CIA agents were in the afternoon sun trying to look through the reflective-tinted glass door. One of them had the weapon on his shoulder. I needed the clothes and Calvin's laptop computer, so swooshing down the sewers wouldn't work.

The first arrow almost passed completely through the agent's neck; the other agent and I could clearly see the arrowhead and half of the shaft protruding through the agent's neck and pointing to the glass door. The agent with the weapon quickly turned to receive two arrows of his own, and both travelled through his neck. I grabbed the computer and phone from the desk.

The screams of afternoon strollers began while the agents were sliding to the ground. Calvin was at the café door with an open umbrella and a bow and arrows on his shoulder. I stepped under the umbrella, but before leaving the doorway, I reached down to the agent and pulled the weapon from his shoulder.

We hurriedly walked to Calvin's black four-door Porsche. I climbed in, and he started the car and pulled away from the café. We left the bodies for the CIA to handle.

* * *

Calvin drove past the convention center as I directed. He was parked a block north of the Hyatt. He was not a minion who asked a lot of questions. He was appreciative of being a minion and for the ownership of the café, but he had a family. He had more loyalties than to me, but his known association with me made him a target for the CIA and slayers. Sending him home to his family could have endangered them, and I needed him.

Using his laptop, I made the hotel reservation for the business suite, then I dialed the number of my vampire banker and reached his secretary.

"He has been trying to reach you for two days. Please hold," his receptionist secretary directed.

The banker answered with, "These are strange times, Ms. Knight. Your father's accounts have been the inquiry of many; rumors that you and sisters are either deceased or human are traveling through our world."

"Yes, I can imagine."

"But stranger still are requests, no ... threats, from the American government to access your accounts. They have been attempting to overstep their authority; trying to bully with a little information, but we are and have been beyond their regulations. Your real worry, at this time, is other vampires inquiring into your father's considerable holdings and concerns."

Vampires were thinking the Knight family was falling apart. They were preparing attacks, hoping we were circling the drain.

"As is our way. Vampires think I have let my father's death happen with no retaliation. They will see different. Rest assured. I am neither human nor deceased, and there will be retribution for my father's death. I am the sole heir to my father's estate; all accounts will be balanced by me. I will be in tomorrow to handle the legal proceedings; today, I need you to arrange a million dollar cash delivery to the Hyatt Convention Center. I am suite 1700, I need it within the hour, and I want you to deliver it personally."

He didn't give me an immediate answer.

"That is a bit out of the ordinary, but no worries. I will be there within the hour. Can I be of service in any other area?"

"No, the cash will suffice."

"What time should I expect you and your attorney tomorrow?"

"8 p.m. works for us."

"8 p.m. it is."

Retribution was no longer a choice; it was mandatory. Jocelyn, the traitor and CIA agent, said she was the new Chad, so I dialed his number hoping to reach her.

"Who is this?" she answered.

"I guess you are the new Chad."

"Melody Knight. I thought you would have fled the country."

"Nope, I am still here."

"Why are you calling the CIA?"

"I'm calling you. I need you to make the Rollins Transportation and Banco Republica presentation to interested parties before the convention."

"It's not going to happen; plans are in place."

"I'll pay you a million in cash."

"Where and when?"

"The convention center, in an hour and fifteen minutes, suite 1700."

I disconnected and dialed my sister's number. When she answered, I told her, "Bring Natalie and Nelson to the Hyatt convention center, suite 1700, now." I disconnected before she could object.

"Ok, Calvin, pull up to the valet. We're good."

* * *

The suite was exactly what I needed; there was a large media screen, a desktop computer, and a large meeting table. Calvin and I were sitting at the table. I still had not told him my plan.

"I'm going to want you to host a meeting."

He nodded yes.

"I am hoping there will representatives from four vampire families, a representative from the CIA, my sister, my daughter, and another young man at the minimum. My sister and my daughter and her friend should arrive first; they are all human."

He made no comment, merely nodding in the affirmative.

"I want you to answer the door with the weapon on and ready and with your pistol visible. The CIA agent, a tall, blond, white woman, should arrive alone. She is being paid for a service, and she is going to want to keep the payment she receives a secret; at least, I think she will.

"The vampires and my banker will probably arrive around the same time. Sit everyone at this table. No one is to leave before my return. The CIA agent will be giving a presentation. Stand armed and ready while she is presenting; the vampires will be disturbed by what she presents. Again, no one leaves until I return. Understand?"

His large frame was rocking in the chair and his big head was nodding. "Yes, Sister Melody. I understand."

I was glad one of us did; my own thoughts were many and scattered. I needed to expose the CIA to Justin Shore and those he brought with him, and I needed to feed, badly; Pike was going to help with that. He was also going to help me demonstrate my strength to challenging vampire families.

"Is there gas in your car?"

"Yes, I filled it up this morning."

"Ok, I'm going to take it. My hope is to be back a little after the guests arrive."

He showed no fear or apprehension. I was more worried than him because the plan in my mind still had many moving parts. I needed to get to Pike, and his death had to be acknowledged by vampires. I couldn't swoosh to him, kill him, and leave because I needed physical proof to show his death. Pike's head would partially demonstrate Knight family retribution.

When I stood from the table, I saw three balls of gas drop from the ceiling vents. Justin Shore materialized up from the carpet right in front of me. Two other gaseous clouds rolled across the floor and materialized in front of the media screen. Five Black male vampires joined us in the suite.

They were early, but I was relieved. Justin Shore could be my witnesses. I could swoosh to Pike and end his life in front of a vampire.

Justin Shore placed his hand on my shoulder. "Your father will be missed." He pointed to each vampire. "Many more wanted to come. To support you, and to assist you. Your father taught you well; we are all witnesses to that. But we all see your family is crumbling."

He stopped talking and each vampire looked to me to respond.

I gestured for Calvin to stand and raise the weapon. "Today, I will show you a threat that attacks us all. This weapon will revert a vampire back to human. The CIA is working with slayers to use it against us. We must show the CIA the error of this association."

The vampire that was moving to the head of the table started laughing. He pulled out a chair and sat. "Why? The pseudo peace has lasted too long. It is time for us to herd the humans like the animals they are. It was only your father who kept us working with them. Let the CIA bring us their war."

I hadn't expected that. His comment was so fearless it shocked me.

"There is no winning such a war," I said.

"Not for the humans," Justin Shore said. He sat at the opposite head of the table.

As the other vampires sat, I got the feeling that the meeting was not going to go as I planned.

The suite door chimed. Calvin lowered the weapon. I directed him to "take a seat," and I went to the door.

Approaching the door, I smelled the earth. I opened the door to see Jocelyn. She didn't greet me, and I didn't greet her.

My banker walked up behind her, and I did greet him warmly. He was dressed in a black three-piece suit with a white shirt and black and gray striped tie. We hugged, and he passed me a thick attaché case. We all walked into the suite toward the table.

Jocelyn walked from the desktop computer to the left table. She did not seem surprised to be in a room full of naked Black male vampires. But what happened next did surprise me.

One more gaseous cloud entered the suite, dropping from the ceiling vent. The cloud transformed into my daughter. I moved as fast as my legs would allow me to Natalie, and we embraced.

Inside my mind she told me, "Aunt Charlotte freed me;

her nurse, her minion, gave me the same pills she gave you." I held my daughter tighter, and it felt good to have her in my thoughts.

"At the hospital, the pills the nurse gave me, they are responsible for me turning back?"

"Yes, Mother. Aunt Charlotte is on our side."

Her words were inside my head and my heart.

Jocelyn beckoned me from the computer. She had inserted her flash drive and was ready to begin the presentation. She looked down at the case in my hand and smiled pleasantly. I handed it to her, and she placed it in the chair in front of her. She cleared her throat and turned to face the room of mostly naked Black male vampires.

"Good afternoon ..." were the last words she spoke.

My daughter was at her neck and feeding in half a second. Natalie dropped to the floor with Jocelyn's body, draining it dry. I picked up my million dollars from the chair while my daughter fed.

I heard the suite door open behind me, and I felt her approaching. Her presence was strong around me. Charlette was back. I waited for her. My vampire sister came and stood by my side.

"Gentlemen, my father was murdered by the CIA, slayers, and vampires." Hanging from her hand was a black backpack with a CIA patch on the pocket. She nodded her head to me and whispered, "Get the weapon from your minion."

Natalie stood up from feeding, and I halfway expected her to belch. I took the weapon from Calvin.

"My niece just killed an undercover slayer. Slayers have infiltrated the CIA, the FBI, and local police across this nation. They are no longer just blind white-eyed swordsmen.

Slayers have evolved, but their purpose remains the same, our destruction."

She unzipped the backpack and dumped Pike's huge head on the table. "This was the CIA director who ordered the murder of my father."

Again, she whispered, "Flip up the switch behind the trigger."

I did, and the weapon powered up for all to hear.

"This human had no offspring, so his line ends with him, but he was a minion to Justin Shore."

She looked at me, but I had already aimed and pulled the trigger. So much gas erupted from the weapon that Justin Shore, his chair, and the area of the table in front of him were covered in red murk, but I kept firing. When I released the trigger, Justin Shore was a human gurgling for air. Calvin handed me his bow with an arrow. I took it, drew, and released. The arrow passed through Justin Shore's chest and the chair he was sitting in.

Charlette told those in the room, "The Knight family stands before you with no enemies."

Whatever plans were brewing among vampires in that room, my sister, my daughter, my minion, and I ended them. We watched vampires swooshing from the suite as if the sun was rolling through it. The only one who didn't flee was my banker. He remained sitting at the table with Pike's head on it. We joined him.

"I am happy you ladies prevailed."

I put the million dollars back into his hands.

"Why?" Natale asked.

We all glanced at the head but made no verbal reference to it.

"The Knight family is vampire tradition. The bank is

only strong because vampires continue to do what they have always done. Mr. Knight, your father, and your grand-father," he looked at each of us respectively, "brought vampire funds together over four hundred years ago. An attack on the Knight family is an attack on vampire tradition, on our history. Your money, your interests belong in our bank." He was looking at Charlette.

"The funds will be returned in the morning," she replied.

He smiled a banker's smile and stood with the case in hand. He nodded his head at us and said, "At your service, ladies." He walked from the suite, leaving us sitting at the table.

Calvin leaned his head toward Justin Shore's human remains and Pike's tabled head and Jocelyn's corpse on the carpet and said, "That's a mess."

Charlette glanced at all three remains then settled her eyes on mine. She tapped the watch on her wrist and without removing her eyes from mine, she said, "Slayer cleanup this location, authorization, Knight 1515."

She looked to Calvin and said, "Nothing we have to worry about."

CHAPTER
- TWENTY -

The waves were consistent, but the darkness made them peaceful. Had the sun been shining, the waves would have been raging. Daniel was remembering, releasing, and informing. I knew he had lived centuries, but his actual living was secret to me.

"During our ravishing and warring, the one who gave me the gift, Yimwen, was persistent in my mind. He begged us to come back to the island and to leave with them for Africa. It was our third night on the mainland when he told me they were leaving, and he was unwavering in his decision to stay. After merely two nights, we had a trunk of gold, pistols and rifles, and paper notes.

"In my mind, Yimwen told me his son wanted to stay,

and he was sending him to us, 'I hope fate is kind to you both'; those were the last words he spoke to me. I never heard Yimwen in my mind again. His son was of the same mindset as Justin; revenge and wealth motivated them.

"It was after a night of pillaging when three unknown vampires walked into the cabin we had commandeered from Portuguese furriers. They didn't swoosh through the doors; they entered dressed as a gentleman, a farmer, and a hunter.

"Outside the cabin was a horse-drawn buggy, a buckboard wagon, and an unsaddled mustang. They did not make requests; they made demands. The hunter spoke first, telling us we should have left with the others, but since we didn't, we had to choose a family to join. Justin told them we were a family. The gentleman's response was to behead Yimwen's son.

The three intruders separated and told us to walk to our choice. Justin and I remained together. The gentleman ordered me to him, and the hunter snatched Justin by his shirt. The cabin filled with over twenty swooshing vampires; they could have easily destroyed us.

"The hunter, farmer, and gentleman divided our bounty between them. They separated into their three represented families and left. It would be sixty years before I saw Justin Shore again. The gentleman was Adam Knight, and he would end a vampire's existence as easily as he did a human's.

"He told me I should have returned with the one that gave me the gift. He believed this greed-filled land would break my soft heart. They had been watching us raid and pillage, and they were disgusted by our actions. They hoped we would die, but when we survived, they had to intervene. We were attracting too much attention from the native people and the colonists.

"Adam Knight did business along the coast; his Dutch and British minions were the faces of his company. I learned how to interact with European businessmen through him, and I learned vampire solidarity from him. He started the first vampire holding company, which became the first vampire bank. But ... he despised his vampire existence. He hated feeding off of humans. He refused to give the living-death to those he fed from. His minions and I made up his family.

"The day he walked into the sun, I inherited over a million dollars. I did what I saw him do; I built coalitions with other vampires. I offered his minions the chance to stay or go independent; once they left, their powers were gone, but they were very wealthy. All of them went out on their own, and they became captains of industry in America and Britain.

"Decades passed before I saw Shore again. His attitude had changed over the years, but he still had a disdain for Europeans; however, I believe white abolitionists expanded his thinking.

"Meeting white people that wanted slavery to end as bad as he did shocked him initially, and eventually freeing slaves and building wealth took protocol over his vengeance. When he saw how badly Africans needed him, he became less self-centered.

"We freed slaves fought in revolts against Britain, built companies, started networks, and funded schools and hospitals all across this nation. We allowed our wealth to help others, vampires and humans. We didn't always see eye-to-eye because he still killed for vengeance. But together, we did more good than bad."

He paused and it was obvious he was waiting for my

response.

"So, you are thinking I am doing more bad than good by keeping the company to myself?"

"I think it would better if you involved other vampires in running the very profitable company. That is what I think."

I didn't look at Daniel. My gaze stayed on the dark waves and their harsh splashing against the pier and rocks. I did what he suggested.

- Monday -

The waitstaff uniform was uncomfortable. I had to pin the skirt in three places to stop it from falling, and the high collared blouse continuously scratched my chin. Nelson was pushing the food cart, and I was serving the steak and chicken breast entrees from it. Natalie was pouring the honored guests water. Walking away from the table, she pulled her dart pen from her apron, and the hand of the guest sitting on the end went to her neck as if she had been bitten by a mosquito.

As I placed the last entrée in front of my target, Nelson's pen was out, and he delivered a dart to a very thin man sipping water. He flinched, but he continued to drink the water. I dropped a fork, which required me to bend down, and while lowered, I delivered two darts to my target's thigh.

I rose and followed Nelson and the cart through the kitchen doors. Others would be serving desert. Charlette and Natalie walked by Nelson, and we followed them to a service elevator. While Nelson was closing the gates and doors, Natalie, Charlette, and I swooshed from the car, leaving the uncomfortable waitstaff uniforms and Nelson behind.

* * *

The three of us were dressing in the same business suite I'd rented earlier. Natalie and I were in the bedroom. I asked her, "Did Nelson say why he didn't take the pill?"

"Yeah, he was quite clear. He wanted to stay human. He didn't understand why I would take it."

"Why did you?"

We both stopped dressing and faced each other. My daughter stood proudly before me, almost at attention like a soldier.

"I am a vampire, Mother. I am Natalie Knight: daughter of Melody Knight and granddaughter of Daniel Knight. Damn," she paused for effect and gave me a big toothy grin, "who wouldn't want to be me?"

She said it so matter-of-factly and with so much pride that I had to give her my own toothy grin.

"So be it," I replied.

CIA Regional Division Head Charlette Knight was standing in the bedroom doorway in a blue business suit with a white shirt and black pumps with two-inch heels. Natalie and I were both in running attire; I was still in my gold Nike running suit and black track shoes.

"Could you guys join us out here?"

By "out here" she meant at the table looking at the large wall-mounted media monitor. And "us" referred to her nurse minion, Nelson, and herself.

Alvin Shore was on the screen and Nelson was talking directly to him.

"Did you have a chance to review the file I sent you?" Nelson asked his brother.

"I did."

"And?"

The screen went blank.

Nelson made several unsuccessful attempts to reconnect. When the video did return, the image on the screen was of a boardroom, and the vampire that was with Justin Shore, the one who laughed at the CIA threat, was sitting next to Alvin Shore. He spoke.

"The relevance of the file escapes us; Rollins Transportation is an international corporation with many holdings. If you are looking to charge us with some type of misconduct, find the appropriate court and do it; other than that, please don't waste our time."

The video feed ended.

"I thought he would listen," Nelson said sadly.

Charlette shook her head to the negative. "No, not today. But our actions downstairs will bring considerable confusion to their corporate dealings." Charlette sounded like the CIA director she'd become.

When Pike gave the weapons to untrained slayers, Charlette reported his actions. Pike's superior was alarmed, but the lack of an investigation into Daniel's death alarmed him more; he had worked with Daniel his whole career.

Looking into Pike's files, it didn't take the superior and Charlette two hours to unravel his deceit. Under the superior's direction, Charlette began observing Pike. The day he shot Moss, she discovered his and Justin Shore's involvement in Daniel's death. Out of reflex, she took the conversion pill and took matters into her own hands. The CIA responded by promoting her to Pike's position.

Charlette looked across the table to Nelson and Natalie and told them, "We can avoid a war, and we will shut down the organ farming; trust me, but it will take a lot of effort from each of us. How this country and how the CIA survives depends on us. The pseudo plans Pike and Jocelyn presented were based in some truth, and we will use parts of them. Yes, there is opposition; those that don't want peace, but maintaining the peace between vampires and humans is a worthy purpose for both humans and vampires. Vampires were once human; neither side can afford to forget that. We are linked."

Hearing Charlette speak made me think of Daniel. So I told her, "You sound like father."

She smiled and nodded her head. "Of course I do, we are Knights."

* * *

When Daniel died, I felt loss and vampire tradition required me to seek retribution, but there was no deep depressing grieving – not even for the one who gave me the gift. But once I returned to being human, grief tore through me.

The deaths of Daniel, Reginald, Marcus, Juanita, and Alexander kept me bedbound and in tears. I needed a vampire's attitude, a vampire's practical thinking, but all I had were human emotions, grief and rage.

Vampires were all human first. Before I became a vampire, I was tired of my human life. My only reason for living had been shot down, murdered in front of me on my wedding day. I was ready to die. But Daniel gave me the living-death, and with that gift my existence took on purpose.

There are those that want the war between vampires and humanity, but there are those like me whose purpose is to keep the peace, to keep the balance.

ABOUT ATMOSPHERE PRESS

Atmosphere Press is an independent, full-service publisher for excellent books in all genres and for all audiences. Learn more about what we do at atmospherepress.com.

We encourage you to check out some of Atmosphere's latest releases, which are available at Amazon.com and via order from your local bookstore:

Twisted Silver Spoons, a novel by Karen M. Wicks
Queen of Crows, a novel by S.L. Wilton
The Summer Festival is Murder, a novel by Jill M. Lyon
The Past We Step Into, stories by Richard Scharine
The Museum of an Extinct Race, a novel by Jonathan Hale Rosen
Swimming with the Angels, a novel by Colin Kersey
Island of Dead Gods, a novel by Verena Mahlow
Cloakers, a novel by Alexandra Lapointe
Twins Daze, a novel by Jerry Petersen
Embargo on Hope, a novel by Justin Doyle
Abaddon Illusion, a novel by Lindsey Bakken
Blackland: A Utopian Novel, by Richard A. Jones
The Jesus Nut, a novel by John Prather
The Embers of Tradition, a novel by Chukwudum Okeke
Saints and Martyrs: A Novel, by Aaron Roe
When I Am Ashes, a novel by Amber Rose
Melancholy Vision: A Revolution Series Novel, by L.C. Hamilton

ABOUT THE AUTHOR

Tony Lindsay is the author of nine novels; *One Dead Preacher, Street Possession, Chasin' It, Urban Affair, One Dead Lawyer, More Boy than Girl, One Dead Doctor, The Killing Breeze, Chess Not Checkers* - and five short story collections titled *Pieces of the Hole - Fat from Papa's Head – Emotional Drippings stories of Love, Lust, and Addiction - Almost Grown – and Acorns in a Skillet stories of Racecraft in America.* He was a contributor to the anthologies: *Revise the Psalm, Don't Hate the Game, Luscious,* and *Fire and Desire.*